ODO HIRSCH was born in A... medicine and worked as a ... London. His books for chil... young and old and have bee... languages.

Praise for Odo Hirsch

'Odo Hirsch's books for children have a zany flavour and wide appeal.' *The Sunday Age*

'Irresistible!' *The Times,* UK

'Strange, delicate, delightful' Philip Pullman, *Guardian*, UK

'Those who love writing and performing plays will treasure *Antonio S and the Mystery of Theodore Guzman,* as will many others who are willing to be entranced by magic in all it's forms... [This story is] something out of the ordinary.' *The Weekend Australian*

'Hazel Green is a memorable character, a child full of ingenuity and determination... Not to be missed!' Jo Goodman, *Magpies*

'*Bartlett and the Ice Voyage* absolutely confirms Hirsch's skills and presages an enduring career for him as a premier children's novelist.' Kevin Steinberger, *Magpies*

LOOK OUT FOR OTHER FAVOURITES
FROM ODO HIRSCH

FOR CHILDREN

Antonio S and the Mystery of Theodore Guzman

Pincus Corbett's Strange Adventure

The Book of Changing Things and Other Oddibosities

Bartlett and the Ice Voyage

Bartlett and the City of Flames

Bartlett and the Forest of Plenty

Bartlett and the Island of Kings

Hazel Green

Something's Fishy, Hazel Green!

Have Courage, Hazel Green!

Think Smart, Hazel Green!

Frankel Mouse

Frankel Mouse and the Bestish Lair

FOR OLDER READERS

Yoss

Slaughterboy

Amelia Dee
and the
peacock lamp

Odo Hirsch

ALLEN&UNWIN

First published in 2007

Allen & Unwin
83 Alexander St
Crows Nest NSW 2065
Australia
Phone: (61 2) 8425 0100
Fax: (61 2) 9906 2218
Email: info@allenandunwin.com
Web: www.allenandunwin.com

National Library of Australia
Cataloguing-in-Publication entry:
Hirsch, Odo.
Amelia Dee and the peacock lamp.

ISBN 9781741753011 (pbk.).

I. Title.

A823.3

Cover design by Design By Committee
Front cover illustration (peacock pattern) by Ali Durham
Back cover illustrations by Elise Hirst (house) and Josh Durham (car)
Set in 10.5pt/16 pt Sabon by Midland Typesetters, Australia
Printed in Australia by Mcphersons Printing Group

10 9 8 7 6 5 4 3

Amelia Dee lived in the green house on Marburg Street. Everyone in the area knew the green house. A plaque above the door said that it had been built by a man called Solomon J Wieszacker, and the date on the plaque was more than a hundred years old.

Solomon J Wieszacker hadn't built the green house with his own two hands, of course, but had paid people to build it for him. Money was no object for Solomon Weiszacker, who had made a fortune importing coffee and exporting coral. He had made a lot of money from red coral, in particular, and quite a lot from yellow coral. Purple coral, to Solomon Weiszacker's surprise, didn't bring in much money at all, and after a while he had stopped dealing in it.

Solomon Weiszacker believed that Marburg Street was going to be a delightful boulevard at the centre of an exclusive suburb, lined with fashionable town houses and attractive shops. This was in the days when the city was growing in all directions, and Marburg Street itself was nothing more than a stretch of road running between empty fields. The city council had just started selling the land alongside it. So Solomon Weiszacker bought a plot about half a kilometre along the stretch of road that had just been laid, with fields on one side and fields on the other, and there he built his house.

It was four storeys high, tall and narrow, as a townhouse should be. Since money was no object to Solomon Weiszacker, no expense was spared. The front of the house was ornamental and elegant. The top floor had a sculpture of a woman seated in a niche between two windows, holding a cup of coffee in one hand and a sprig of coral in the other, looking down over the street. The walls at the sides of the house, however, were blank, without a single window or any decoration, because Solomon was sure that one day the land along Marburg Street would be so expensive that the town houses would stand literally wall to wall. Behind the house was a long garden that Solomon enclosed by building a fence to separate it from the fields all around.

When the house was finished, Solomon Weiszacker put the plaque above the door and the entire front of the house, even the sculpted lady, was painted green, which was his favourite colour. But the side walls were left as bare, grey brick, because Solomon was certain that soon they would be obscured by the other tall, fashionable town houses that were sure to be built on either side.

Things didn't turn out quite as Solomon Weiszacker expected. For some reason, wealthy people went to live in other parts of the growing city, and the houses that sprang up along Marburg Street, instead of being tall and fashionable, were small and ordinary, only a single storey high. They had shops in the front and living areas in the back. Eventually they ran from one end of Marburg Street to the other, and the green house stood alone amongst them, rising four storeys up, like a tree that had been planted by mistake in the middle of a hedge, with the bare, windowless walls at the sides visible for all the world to see.

After Solomon Weiszacker died, the green house was sold, and sold again, and one family after another lived in it. Each family left its mark, knocking down walls inside, or building them up, putting in cupboards and installing fittings, or taking them out, according to their needs. At some point the ground floor had been turned into a shop, with its own door and a big curved window on the street. But no matter what else was done to it, the front of the house was always painted green. Originally it had been a kind of sea green, but this was very faded by the time old Solomon Weiszacker died. Then it was olive green, and for a brief time it was lemon green, and then it was lime green, and there was even a period when it was emerald green. The general opinion in Marburg Street in those days was that emerald green was far too bright and preposterous for the old house of Solomon Weiszacker, and there was a general sense of relief when a new family moved in and repainted it a respectable myrtle green. Yet no one ever painted the front any colour but green, nor did anyone ever paint the bare brick walls at the side, or even seem to consider it.

Amelia couldn't remember living in any other house. Her parents had bought it when she was one, and very few people, if any, can remember anything from before they're one, and Amelia Dee wasn't one of them. The green house was far too large for a family with only a single child, of course, but Amelia's mother, who was of an artistic temperament, had fallen in love with it. She had a room for her painting, and a room for her weaving, and a room in which to make her sculptures, most of which ended up in the long, narrow garden behind the house. At the back of the garden was a big shed, which was perfect for Amelia's father, who was of an inventive temperament.

There was a housekeeper, as well, whose name was Mrs Ellis. She didn't live in the green house, but she almost might as well have, considering how much time she spent there. She did not only the housekeeping, but the shopping, the cooking, and everything else that Amelia's mother and father were too busy to do. Which was just about everything. Mrs Ellis and Amelia's mother frequently got into fierce arguments. When Amelia was smaller, she had been terrified that after one of these fights her mother might tell Mrs Ellis to go away and never come back, or Mrs Ellis might decide not to come back even without being told, and then who would do everything that needed to be done? But as she got older, Amelia realised that nothing ever came of these fights, and she learned to ignore them, just as her father did.

As a young man, Amelia's father had made a fortune from a powder he had invented that made everyone sneeze, even when applied in only minute amounts. He hadn't been trying to invent a powder to make people sneeze – which was hardly necessary, considering how often people sneeze by themselves – but that was what he had ended up doing. To the surprise of everyone, including Amelia's father, the powder turned out to be incredibly irritating not only to human noses but to ants, cockroaches, earwigs, silverfish and members of the insect kingdom in general. A single sprinkling of the powder could clear an entire building. It was very fortunate there were so many ants, cockroaches, earwigs and silverfish to be got rid of, Amelia often thought, because she had no idea what her father would have done if he hadn't made a fortune from his powder and had had to hold down a regular job for a living. As for inventing, he had never produced anything remotely as useful again. That didn't stop him trying. The house was cluttered with contraptions and mechanisms that he had installed, removed, 'improved' and reinstalled, usually a number of times.

Across the stairs, for instance, ran a series of almost invisible wires. They were the relic of an idea Amelia's father had for stopping people getting hurt if they fell downstairs. The wires were connected to sensors, and if one of the sensors detected a heavy blow on a stair, as if someone was falling, big balloon-like bags were supposed to suddenly inflate from all over the place – under the stairs, beside the stairs, on the landings – to cushion the fall. There was nothing wrong with the theory, it was only the practice that created problems. The bags had an unfortunate habit of inflating without warning, and without the slightest blow being detected. The sight of twenty big orange balloons suddenly bursting out all over the stairs was enough to give anyone a fright, even Mrs Ellis, and make her drop the soup, or whatever else she was carrying. Not to mention the fourteen times – because Mrs Ellis counted – that a bag had simply blown up as she passed by and bowled her over. Or the fact that Amelia, who was younger then, had a habit of stamping on the stairs to make the bags inflate and then throwing herself into them. She just didn't have a habit of admitting she had done it. Eventually Mrs Ellis demanded that Amelia's father dismantle the system. No, he couldn't 'improve' it, she insisted, he had 'improved' it enough! Either it went, or she did. He took out the balloons, but vowed that he would perfect the system, whatever Mrs Ellis said, and left the wires in readiness. But some other invention took his attention, as often happened, and then another, and another, and the perfection of this particular one had been left for later, together with so many other half-finished devices that needed completion. So the wires remained, and over time they had worked themselves loose and become a trap to trip people over, and the invention, which had been designed to keep people safe, had ended up doing exactly the opposite.

Yet the most interesting thing in the house, for Amelia, had nothing to do with her father's inventions. It was a large, exceptionally intricate metalwork lamp that hung at the top of the stairs. The lamp was one of the things that had been installed at some point and then left behind when one family moved out and another moved in, and no one could say where it had come from or when. It hung outside the door to Amelia's room, which was on the top floor, just beyond the banister. Every time she went in or out of her room, Amelia passed it. No one else in the house knew the lamp as Amelia did. No one else knew the secrets that were contained within it, the extraordinary things that the lamp's creator had hidden within the fine details of its metalwork.

Amelia kept them to herself, or at most, she shared them with the one other person whom she knew would never utter a word of what she told her. That person was right outside her window. If Amelia leaned out, she could see the face of the sculpted lady with the coffee and the coral who sat at the top of the front of the house, not more than two metres away from her.

The sculptor who created the lady had given her no eyes, but only blank surfaces between her eyelids. You couldn't tell this from the street, but you could see it when you were this close to her. In a way, it made Amelia sad to think that all the time the lady had been sitting there she had been blind. It would have made it so much easier for her to pass the time – and she had been there more than a hundred years, which is a lot of time to pass

– if she could at least have watched what was happening in Marburg Street. But then Amelia would imagine that the lady, even though she was blind, had some other, mysterious way of knowing what was happening below her, a way that was more powerful than merely seeing, and that everything was stored up in her memory. Sometimes Amelia imagined the stories the sculpted lady could have told, if only she could have spoken, about all the things that had happened in Marburg Street since the day Solomon J Wieszacker put up the plaque above the door on the ground floor. Sometimes, when Amelia leaned out of the window and looked down at the street, she would murmur something to the lady about what was happening down there, almost as if she expected to hear the lady's opinion in response. And sometimes she imagined that she could tell what the lady was thinking by the expression she saw in her face – a hint of amusement, a cloud of concern – even though she knew that the lady's features were carved in stone.

When Amelia looked straight down, she could see the bulge of the curved window at the front of the shop on the ground floor. But if you went down to the street, you couldn't see anything through the glass. For years, and certainly for as long as Amelia could remember, a kind of big white sheet had hung behind the window, obscuring the view of whatever might be happening inside.

And the only clue that anything, in fact, might be happening in there was a small handwritten sign taped inside the glass. The sign had been there for years as well, and the tape that held it was yellow with age.

In faded red letters, very neatly written, was a name.

LK Vishwanath.

CHAPTER 2

There were all kinds of rumours about Mr Vishwanath and what he was up to behind the sheet in the ground-floor window of the green house on Marburg Street. According to some people, he was a kind of a dervish, and went into trances standing on one leg and not eating for months at a time. Or he was some kind of crime boss, according to others, with a secret communications network and a room stashed full of money, but the police could never prove anything against him. And those were only some of the rumours. Most of Amelia's friends were quite frightened of him. He rarely came out of his shop, and some of Amelia's friends had never seen him at all. They were the most frightened of the lot. Amelia, on the other hand, saw him often, not in the street at the front of the house, but in the garden behind it.

She would look out the window of her mother's weaving room on the third floor, and Mr Vishwanath would be in the garden, amongst the sculptures in the grass, wearing nothing but a piece of shiny clothing that was like a kind of big blue nappy. He would be

11

standing on one leg, with the other foot wrapped around his neck, or kneeling with his back arched and the top of his head touching the ground behind him, or holding some other pose that Amelia couldn't have held if her life depended on it. She knew, because sometimes she tried. She would twist herself into the shape he had assumed, or start to, but she always ended up keeling over on the floor of the weaving room before she managed to get her foot anywhere near around the back of her neck, or the top of her head on the ground, or whatever Mr Vishwanath seemed to be doing with such ease in the garden below her. When she got herself up again and looked out, Mr Vishwanath would still be there, holding the pose perfectly, as still and as steady as one of the sculptures around him, with his eyes closed and the dark skin of his tall, thin body gleaming in the sunlight.

The truth was that Mr Vishwanath was a master of yoga. The room behind the sheet on the ground floor was the studio where he taught, and he lived in the back part of the shop behind it.

Amelia had no idea how old Mr Vishwanath was. He had perfectly white hair, which should have meant he was very old, yet there was barely a wrinkle on his face, which should have meant he was somewhat younger. Sometimes, when he wasn't practising yoga and he wasn't teaching, he would come out in a faded red shirt and a pair of old trousers, and sit in a chair that he had put under the verandah at the back of the house. It was an old, battered chair, and tufts of stuffing poked out from tears in the upholstery. Mr Vishwanath liked to sit there on warm days, for hours, sometimes, just looking at the garden, with an expression that wasn't quite a smile, yet seemed to have some kind of deep contentment in it. Once Amelia decided to see what was so special about sitting there and staring at the garden, and she sat down under the verandah, beside him. Mr Vishwanath didn't seem to mind. Then Amelia brought down a chair and put it next to Mr Vishwanath's chair, and sometimes, when she saw him there, she would come and sit there as well. Not for hours, but for a while. There was something peaceful about sitting there with Mr Vishwanath. You could smell the sweet scent of the oil he put on before he practised his yoga. He didn't expect you to talk, and you could just sit beside him and think your own thoughts – which is an unusual thing to be able to do, if you stop to consider it, when you're with somebody else. But if she wanted to talk, she could, and Mr Vishwanath didn't stop her. He just didn't necessarily reply, and if he did, you didn't know when he was going to do it. It might be ten minutes after you'd said whatever he was replying to, and you'd almost forgotten you'd said it.

The only problem, thought Amelia, was that Mr Vishwanath had too much time to sit there. He had very few students. Once or twice a week an old lady would arrive in a large, cream-coloured car, driven by a man in a uniform who would wait outside while the lady was in Mr Vishwanath's studio. Everyone knew about her, because you could hardly miss her grand arrival or the sight of the driver waiting for her, although there were suspicions about whether she was there for yoga or for some other reason connected with Mr Vishwanath's supposedly mysterious activities. From time to time someone else would ring the bell beside the door on the ground floor, but not very often. And if there were other students, Amelia didn't know about them. It never once occurred to Amelia that this lack of students was because Mr Vishwanath wasn't a good teacher. Anyone who could do the poses he performed in the back garden must be a true master of yoga. But how were people supposed to know what he could do, with only one tiny sign on the window of his studio and only Mr Vishwanath's name on the sign?

Anyone could see that Mr Vishwanath wasn't rich. In fact, Amelia suspected he was quite poor. And yet she was sure he was an excellent teacher, and could have made a lot of money, if only people knew about him.

'You should advertise, Mr Vishwanath,' she said to him. 'People just don't know what you do.'

It wasn't the first time Amelia had said that. Mr Vishwanath turned to look at her, and didn't reply.

'It's just a suggestion,' said Amelia.

Mr Vishwanath continued to look at her, as if considering the idea. Then he gazed at the garden again.

'I could write the advertisement for you, if you like,' said Amelia. 'You could put it in the newspaper. And I'll make you a sign, for your shop. A big sign, saying YOGA.'

Amelia watched Mr Vishwanath's face. A slight frown came over it at mention of the big sign saying YOGA, and then it was gone.

She could just imagine the sign she would make. She would write YOGA in big gold letters, and underneath it she would draw a picture of Mr Vishwanath in one of his poses, maybe the one where he stood on one leg with his other foot hooked around his neck. Amelia wasn't sure she could draw a really good picture of Mr Vishwanath, but she thought that if she waited until he came out into the back garden, and then sketched him when he was standing there with his eyes closed, she might get it right. On the other hand, she could have asked her mother for help, but Amelia didn't want to do that, because her mother would take over the whole thing and turn it into one of her artistic projects and poor old Mr Vishwanath would end up with some huge

15

artistic painting in his window. Besides, Amelia didn't really think her mother could draw people very well. The eyes in her pictures were never quite level, or the ears were too high, or there was something else that wasn't right about the faces she painted, although her father praised every picture she did as if it was the next *Mona Lisa*. He was always asking people who came to the house what they thought of the pictures, which hung all over the walls. There was always a minute or two when they stammered and frowned while they thought of something to say.

No, Mr Vishwanath needed a nice, simple sign. Below the picture of him doing his one-legged pose, she would write LK Vishwanath, and under that she would write Yoga Master, or maybe Yoga Maestro, which sounded more important. And under that she would write New Students Wanted. Or maybe New Students Welcome, which sounded less desperate.

Amelia nodded to herself, staring at the garden. She could see the sign in her mind's eye. In fact, perhaps she'd just go ahead and make it for Mr Vishwanath. When he saw it, he'd realise how much better it would be if he had the sign in his window.

'Amelia, this is not the way.'

Amelia looked around. Mr Vishwanath had a deep, quiet voice, like a purr, and when he first started talking sometimes you weren't certain whether the sound was coming from him or from inside your own head.

'What's not the way, Mr Vishwanath?' asked Amelia.

'This is not the way for students to come to yoga. They must come because they are drawn. They must come because they have the need.'

'But they may not realise they have the need. If you put up a nice big sign, they'll realise.'

'No,' said Mr Vishwanath. 'This is not the way.'

'Then what is the way?' asked Amelia.

'The way is the way it is now,' replied Mr Vishwanath.

The way it is now, thought Amelia. One little sign that was so small you couldn't even see it from the other side of the street, and with so little information that you wouldn't know what it meant even if you did see it. Amelia crossed her arms in frustration. 'You're just saying that because you don't like anything to change, Mr Vishwanath. You only like the old ways.'

Mr Vishwanath didn't reply.

'You don't want to try anything new.'

Mr Vishwanath shook his head. 'Not so, Amelia. In my youth I was a great enthusiast for things that were new. There was nothing that I did not try.'

Amelia looked at Mr Vishwanath doubtfully. It was hard to imagine Mr Vishwanath being young, let alone being a great enthusiast for things that were new. Whatever that was supposed to mean.

'In some cases, ways that are new may be good. But in other cases, the ways that are old are better.'

'Well, if you ask me, Mr Vishwanath, in this case, the old way doesn't seem to be working.'

'On the contrary,' replied Mr Vishwanath. 'It is working perfectly.' He turned his gaze at the garden again.

On the contrary? Amelia shook her head. Mr Vishwanath had a funny way of measuring whether something was working!

There was silence.

'I would rather have one true student than a hundred followers,' said Mr Vishwanath quietly.

Amelia frowned. She had heard Mr Vishwanath say that before. But he'd change his mind if he saw the sign she had in mind. She looked at him. No, she thought, he wouldn't.

Amelia gazed at the garden as well. It was full of sculptures, her mother's latest, which Amelia's father had lowered from the window of the sculpture room with a special winch he had invented. They were all white sculptures, about a metre tall, and very narrow, and they were supposed to represent long thin faces on long thin necks. This was because Amelia's mother was going through a Linear Phase, according to Amelia's father. Prior to her Linear Phase, Amelia's mother had spent a year making dark, squat, rounded sculptures, like foaming bubbles of mud. That meant she had been in a Globular Phase. Now the bubble sculptures were all piled down the very back of the garden, together with the sculptures from all the earlier phases Amelia's mother had been through. When one of her phases was over, Amelia's mother couldn't bear to look at the sculptures again, and Amelia's father would stack them at the end of the garden, out of view, and replace them with the pieces Amelia's mother produced when she went into a new phase. Amelia's mother went through phases in her paintings as well. There had been the Blue Phase, when everything was painted in shades of blue, and the Red Phase, and the Yellow Phase. Her latest phase was a Multicoloured Phase, with numerous colours jostling loudly in every painting. Some of those paintings had so many colours they made you feel quite ill.

Amelia stared at the white, thin sculptures that poked up out of the long grass. The only place her mother would allow her sculptures to be placed was inside the four high walls of the garden. Once, when her father had suggested she should have an exhibition, she hadn't talked to him for a week.

Amelia couldn't see the point of all the work that went into the sculptures if they were just going to be put in the garden. Whenever her father had finished positioning a new sculpture there, he always said it didn't matter whether anyone saw it, all that mattered was that her mother had expressed herself. But Amelia wasn't so sure. She didn't really believe that could be all that mattered, even for her mother. Amelia didn't think her mother was very brave, hiding her sculptures in the garden where no one would see them.

'Why do you think she keeps making them?' murmured Amelia, as much to herself as Mr Vishwanath.

Mr Vishwanath glanced at Amelia with an expression that wasn't quite a smile. Or perhaps it was. 'Don't you know?' he said.

Amelia shook her head. Mr Vishwanath watched her for a moment longer, and then gazed at the sculptures again.

CHAPTER 3

Amelia's best friend was Eugenie Edelstein, and her other best friend was Kevin Chan. Eugenie was a lot harder on Mr Vishwanath than Kevin.

'It's his own fault if he won't advertise,' said Eugenie. 'How many students does he have?'

'A few,' said Amelia, feeling as if she had to defend Mr Vishwanath.

'A few? There's the old lady who comes with the driver in the big car, that's the only one I can think of, and who knows what she really does there?'

There were all kinds of rumours about what the lady really did when she went into Mr Vishwanath's studio. Few people believed she could possibly be going there simply to do yoga. Kids who thought the place was some kind of a front, and Mr Vishwanath must be a spy master or a crime boss, thought the mysterious woman's appearance was proof of their theory. She must be someone who carried messages for Mr Vishwanath, or brought him instructions, or delivered money, or something else, and her driver was some kind of bodyguard. Others objected that she was too

21

old to be a crime messenger or a money deliverer. Exactly, said the kids who thought she was. That was the whole point. Who would suspect an old lady like that? She was perfect for the job, whatever it actually was.

Amelia murmured something about other students coming, lots of other students.

'Well, if he really wants more students, and he won't even put up a sign,' declared Eugenie, 'he has no one to blame but himself.'

'Is he blaming anyone?' asked Kevin.

Amelia shook her head.

'I was speaking figuratively,' said Eugenie, in a rather pompous tone. Eugenie had a tendency to pomposity. Her mother, who had a tendency to pomposity as well, and loved everything French, had named her after some long-dead French empress, and told Eugenie that she should never forget it. Whatever that was supposed to mean. Eugenie's outbursts of pomposity made Amelia and Kevin laugh. When they laughed, Eugenie just became even more pompous.

They laughed.

Eugenie put her nose in the air. 'If one can't speak figuratively, I hardly know why one bothers,' she muttered to herself.

Amelia and Kevin glanced at each other and grinned.

Eugenie walked along with her nose even further in the air. One day, thought Amelia, she'd be walking along like that and she'd trip over something.

'I don't think advertising is Mr Vishwanath's problem,' said Kevin. 'In fact, I've heard he knocks students back.' Kevin looked at Amelia meaningfully, as if to remind her again of the rumours that Mr Vishwanath wasn't running a yoga studio at all behind the sheet in his window, but something altogether more mysterious and sinister, and that the old lady was somehow involved in it.

'So have I,' said Eugenie, lowering her nose and looking at Amelia in exactly the same insinuating way.

Amelia stopped. 'How do you know?'

'Everyone knows,' replied Eugenie. 'My mother has a friend whose sister's niece had a second cousin who wanted to learn yoga from Mr Vishwanath, and when she went—'

'Wait a minute,' said Kevin, 'can you just run through that again to make sure we've got it? Your mother's friend's sister . . .'

'*When* she went to Mr Vishwanath,' said Eugenie sternly, throwing a disapproving glance at Kevin, 'he told her to go to the Fitness Fanatics gym and learn yoga there.'

'Why?' asked Amelia.

'I have no idea,' replied Eugenie. 'She was quite insulted.'

'What did she do?'

'She went to Fitness Fanatics. She said she can learn just as much at Fitness Fanatics. The people are nicer, and they don't tell her to go away. She said she doesn't need any old Mr Vishwanath to tell her what to do.'

Kevin laughed.

'What's funny about that?' demanded Eugenie.

'Well, she said she didn't need Mr Vishwanath to tell her what to do, and then she did exactly what Mr Vishwanath told her . . .' Kevin stopped. There wasn't the slightest sign on Eugenie's face that she saw the irony. 'Doesn't matter,' he murmured.

Eugenie turned back to Amelia. 'In her opinion, Mr Vishwanath is too big for his boots.'

Amelia had never seen Mr Vishwanath in boots. He wore slippers when he sat in his chair under the back verandah, and sandals if he left the house to go shopping, whatever the weather. And he didn't wear any kind of shoes when he stood on one foot amongst the sculptures in the back garden and put his other foot behind his neck.

They went into the Sticky Sunday ice-cream shop. Kevin got a double scoop of Starfruit and Pistachio. Amelia got Blueberry Ripple and Peaches 'n' Cream. Eugenie spent ten minutes examining every flavour and then got a small serve of plain frozen yoghurt. They sat down on the stools along the wall.

'That's very peculiar,' murmured Amelia, as she licked the Blueberry Ripple.

'No it's not,' snapped Eugenie. 'I can have frozen yoghurt if I like.'

'No,' said Amelia. 'I mean what you were saying about Mr Vishwanath. She glanced at Kevin. 'You're saying you've heard he knocks people back as well?'

Kevin nodded.

Amelia frowned. She turned her ice-cream cone and thoughtfully licked the Peaches 'n' Cream. This was the first she had heard of Mr Vishwanath sending people away. It didn't sound like something he would do. He never sent her away when she came down to sit with him under the verandah, and she wasn't even a yoga student. Yet according to both Eugenie and Kevin, that was what he did, and everyone knew it. *And* he wouldn't advertise. This was no good. Amelia turned the cone again, still thinking. This was no good at all.

Mr Vishwanath chuckled when Amelia told him what Eugenie had said about the lady who came to learn yoga. He chuckled even more when Amelia told him she had gone to Fitness Fanatics.

'She says she can learn just as much there as she could learn from you, Mr Vishwanath!'

Mr Vishwanath didn't reply.

'The people are nicer, and they don't tell her to go away.'

'I didn't tell her to go away,' said Mr Vishwanath.

'What did you tell her?'

Mr Vishwanath sighed. 'I told her she might be happier at Fitness Fanatics.'

'It's the same thing, isn't it?' said Amelia.

Mr Vishwanath shook his head. 'No, Amelia. It isn't the same thing at all.'

Amelia frowned. It was almost the same thing. And even if it wasn't, it certainly wasn't a way of making the lady feel welcome.

'Anyway,' said Mr Vishwanath. 'She's happy at Fitness Fanatics, isn't she?'

Amelia shrugged. 'I suppose so.'

'Well?' said Mr Vishwanath, and he looked at Amelia for a moment longer, then turned to gaze at the thin white sculptures in the garden.

Amelia stole a glance at him. The expression on Mr Vishwanath's face was perfectly calm, as if he wasn't disturbed by anything, and least of all by the lady who had gone to Fitness Fanatics. But he was never going to get any more students if he kept doing things like that. He'd have only that one old lady who turned up in her cream-coloured car, presuming she really was a yoga student and not something else altogether.

'Eugenie Edelstein says you send lots of people away,' said Amelia.

Mr Vishwanath didn't reply.

'Kevin Chan said so as well. They can't both be wrong.'

Amelia waited for Mr Vishwanath to say something.

'Is that true, Mr Vishwanath?' she asked eventually.

There was silence.

'I would rather have one true student than a hundred followers,' said Mr Vishwanath softly.

'What does that mean, Mr Vishwanath?' said Amelia.

Mr Vishwanath didn't reply.

Amelia jumped up in frustration. She felt like kicking over all the sculptures in the garden with their thin white faces and their thin white necks.

Instead, she went inside. In the kitchen, Mrs Ellis was mixing something in a bowl. Amelia went straight past her and up the stairs.

CHAPTER 4

Amelia had been fascinated by the lamp at the top of the stairs from the moment she had been old enough to be fascinated by anything. From the bottom of the stairwell, four storeys below, the lamp didn't look so big, and it was only when you were at the top that you realised how large it really was. It hung from the ceiling by three chains. The middle of the lamp had six sides, in each of which was clasped a glass panel, and the cone-shaped top and bottom were fashioned entirely out of bronze. The metalwork flowed with intricate patterns and there were hundreds of tiny spaces out of which the light filtered in a wonderful, stippled, hazy glow. Even when she was small, Amelia would stare at the lamp, certain there must be something to find in the apparently endless, swirling patterns of bronze. But it was only when she realised there was a way to get closer to the lamp that she discovered what it was.

The way Amelia found to get closer was to get up on the banister, just at the point where it ended at the wall, holding onto the door frame of her room with one hand to steady herself. From here, she could see the lamp a lot better, and even reach out and touch it. She was quite small when she worked out how to do this, but not so small that she didn't know that if her parents saw her standing on the banister, reaching out and turning the lamp, they'd think she was going to fall over the edge. So she never did it when they could see her. But she did it.

Later, after she had discovered the secrets that the metalwork of the lamp contained, Amelia sometimes imagined she was the only person in the whole world who knew them. Otherwise, she imagined, the secrets had gone to the grave with the lamp's creator. And whether this was true or not, she was certainly the only person in the world who knew that she had almost died because of the lamp. Or that she had secretly begun to write stories because of it.

Amelia's discovery of the lamp's secrets began soon after she started standing on the banister. One day, as she was turning the lamp, she thought she recognised a shape in the metalwork of the bottom. Then it was gone. She stopped turning the lamp and looked for it. Where? Suddenly she found it again. It was like a bird's head. Quite small. There was its beak. Then its neck. She followed it. A body. Feathers, with circles, fronds. A huge fan of feathers. Suddenly Amelia realised what she was looking at. A peacock! She turned the lamp.

There was another! In fact, the entire bottom of the lamp was made up of this pair of peacocks. Amelia discovered that what she had imagined to be a swirling, meaningless pattern, or maybe some kind of field of flowers, was actually a pair of magnificent, fanning peacock tails.

After that, Amelia found there were things to discover everywhere. She would stand on the banister, turning the lamp, peering at the metalwork around the glass panels. At first you would discern nothing, even things that you had already discovered, and you would just see patterns, swirls. Then you would notice a shape, like a tiny clue, and you would follow it, and suddenly the picture would reveal itself. A clawed paw led to a tiger that prowled across the top of one of the glass faces. A curling tail led to a monkey, and then to another, and another, and suddenly you had found a whole string of monkeys tumbling and chasing each other around another one of the panels. There was a heron. A rhinoceros. Birds, animals, flowers, dolphins. And people. Tiny figures that looked like clowns, others that wore a strange, twisting kind of hat. And there were apparently little jokes included. One of the monkeys had a devilish human face. The heron was looking for a fish that was swimming just behind it. One of the hats was actually a snail. Tiny frogs and lizards poked their tongues out in the most unlikely places. Yet the most amazing thing – more amazing than any of the details in the metalwork – was that whoever had made the lamp, whoever had created these details, must have known that it would almost certainly hang too high for anyone to see them. And yet still the lampmaker had created them.

Then, one day, Amelia found something else.

She was standing on the banister, turning the lamp, when she noticed two tiny hinges, so cleverly incorporated in the metalwork that they were almost invisible. They were at the edge of one of the six glass panels, and at the other edge of the panel, she noticed, was a very narrow gap. Not a lock, or a lever, just the tiniest, thinnest gap. If you slid something into the gap, and pulled back, Amelia realised, the panel would swing open at the hinges. It was a door that opened into the lamp.

But she would need both hands to do it, one to hold the lamp steady and the other to slide something into the gap. And if she used two hands, she wouldn't be able to steady herself against the frame of her door while she stood on the banister. Yet there had to be a way to do it.

She got a piece of rope. She waited until her mother was in her painting room, and her father was in his invention shed, and Mrs Ellis was out getting the groceries. She tied one end of the rope around her ankle and the other end around the banister. Then she climbed up on the banister, holding onto the door frame, and she pulled a little knife out of her pocket – the smallest and thinnest she had been able to find in the kitchen – and then, very slowly, she let go of the door frame.

At that instant, as she balanced on the banister at the top of the stairwell, with one hand on the lamp and the other holding the knife, Amelia felt an amazing kind of lightness. It was as if she had left the earth behind. The world seemed to stop.

Then she began to wobble. Suddenly the banister under her feet seemed slippery and round. Instinctively, she grabbed for the lamp with both hands, and as she did, she toppled. The knife plunged to the bottom of the stairs. And Amelia Dee dangled in the air above the stairwell, holding on to the bronze lamp.

The lamp swung out, taking her with it. The chains groaned. The lamp swung back, then out again, then back. Amelia saw the banister coming towards her and she lunged. Over the top she went. She landed on one knee with a thud.

Her heart pounded. The lamp was still swinging. Amelia poked her nose between the banisters and looked down. The knife was a tiny glint of light at the bottom of the stairs.

The rope was still around her ankle. Amelia reached for it and the knot unravelled in her hand. She realised what would have happened if she had lost her grip on the lamp, or if the chains had given way.

Amelia didn't tell anyone about the incident, not even Eugenie or Kevin. When people asked why she was limping, she said she'd tripped over. Even now, years later, no one knew she had swung from the lamp above the stairs, and what would have happened if the lamp hadn't been strong enough to hold her.

It was a scary experience. But an interesting one. Amelia imagined what might have resulted if she really had plunged to the bottom of the stairs, she and the lamp. For a start, Mrs Ellis would have found her there when she came in with the groceries. Amelia would have been dead, of course, and she imagined what everyone would have done. Tears. Grief. Accusations. 'If only you had been watching her.' 'No, if only *you* had!' Maybe she would come back as a ghost, as often happened in the horror books she loved reading. Maybe she would haunt the house. Maybe she would meet the ghost of old Solomon Weiszacker, who probably haunted the house as well. She wondered what kind of a ghost old Solomon Weiszacker would be. Probably a disappointed one, seeing as he had obviously made a big mistake about the kind of houses that were going to be built in Marburg Street. It didn't take much to get Amelia's imagination going, far less than this. Ideas always seemed to be popping up in her head about things that had happened or might have happened or should have happened, often of the most extraordinary nature.

Most of the time, Amelia herself didn't know where her ideas came from. Sometimes she turned them into stories. Everyone thought she was reading when she was in her room, and often she was reading, but not always. Sometimes she was writing.

Amelia had whole drawers full of the stories she had written. Some of them went back years, and were in the big childish writing she had when she was smaller. She couldn't remember exactly why she had started. Her mother, with her painting and her sculpting and her weaving, seemed to do everything else. Maybe that had something to do with it. Amelia couldn't remember exactly when she had started, either, but it was after she swung on the lamp. She had never actually written down the story about how she had swung and crashed to the ground and was found by Mrs Ellis and met Solomon Weiszacker's disappointed ghost, but it was vivid in her mind, every word of it. And it must have been shortly after this happened – or would have happened had the lamp not been strong enough to hold her – that she did start writing down her stories and putting them away in drawers, first in one drawer, then another, which were now full of the things she had written.

Amelia always made sure the door of her room was closed when she was writing. She had never told anyone about the stories, apart from the sculpted lady outside her window, who knew all her secrets. Sometimes Amelia had a feeling that writing stories was a slightly silly thing to do, and other people would laugh if they knew. She wrote stories at school, of course, like everyone else, but they didn't count because the teachers made everyone do it. All the kids were always laughing about a boy in Amelia's class called Martin Martinez, who wrote stories in his spare time and brought them to school where he loved to read them out and was always trying to get them into the school magazine. Everyone said he thought he was some kind of a new Charles Dickens or William Shakespeare or something. Most of Martin Martinez's stories had something to do with Argentina, which was where his family came from. Privately, Amelia thought her stories were much better than the ones Martin Martinez wrote. And he was a terrible boaster, and didn't seem to realise that the more he boasted about his stories, the more everyone laughed at him. Yet Amelia couldn't help admiring him just a little, despite herself, for showing his stories to the world.

The lamp was always giving Amelia ideas, and not only about what would happen if she plunged to her death and came back as a ghost. She often wondered where the lamp came from. From its size alone it was obvious that it must have been intended to hang in a very large room, and from its beauty that it must have been designed for a place of great elegance and luxury. Amelia's favourite story about the lamp was that it had once hung in a faraway palace, long before the days when there was electricity, and there had been oil burning inside it, and every evening a servant would come with a ladder and open the little door and replenish the oil in the lamp. Naturally, there was a princess in the story, and the light hung in her room. The princess loved a handsome young man, who was a gardener, or sometimes he was a guardsman, or sometimes he was a metalworker, but in the story he was never a prince, and her parents, the king and the queen – whose name was sometimes Eugenie, especially if Amelia was thinking of the story on a day when Eugenie Edelstein had been particularly pompous – wouldn't let her marry him. They sent the handsome young man away. The princess became very sad, and wouldn't eat, and refused to leave her room. And as a protest, she refused to allow the lamp to be lit. So the door to the lamp, which had been opened every evening, remained closed, as the princess pined for her lover.

Then the story had different endings. Amelia had never written them down, but they were all in her head.

Sometimes the king and queen relented, and they allowed the handsome young man to come back, and the princess and the young man were married, and the lamp was lit again every night. That was quite a soppy ending, almost a fairy tale, and Amelia felt guilty for even thinking of it. But sometimes that really was the ending she preferred, when she was in a soppy mood. Other times, the king and queen forced the princess to marry a horrible, nasty prince, and they became king and queen in their turn, and grew old, and eventually the nasty husband died, and the princess was left, although now she was a lonely old queen, and one day an old man arrived at the palace, and it was the handsome young man who had been driven away so many years before, and even though it was so many years since they had seen each other, and they had both grown old, they recognised each other at once, and as they kissed, the lamp, which still had a little oil left from all those years before, burst into light once more, but as soon as they had kissed, they died in each other's arms, and the light sputtered out forever. But that was still fairly soppy, although at least they both died. Sometimes, when they kissed, they became young again, and they lived happily ever after, which was even soppier. So sometimes, the handsome man wasn't allowed back, and the princess didn't marry a nasty prince, but pined away in her room, and died of sadness, and the lamp never glowed again. And sometimes, after she had died, the ghost of the princess came back, and the animals on the lamp sprang to life as phantom beasts, vicious, bloodthirsty, and would obey nobody but the ghost-princess, who had no sadness now, but demanded vengeance. There was no end of bloodcurdling things that could be done in that big palace when the ghost-princess came back in the night with her phantom tigers and monkeys and rhinoceroses and other beasts – much more scary and bloodcurdling than anything Amelia ever read in her horror books – and sometimes Amelia had to stop imagining them before she frightened herself so much that she wouldn't be able to sleep.

Funnily enough, after a while, Amelia had found that she was glad she hadn't succeeded in opening the lamp, but had only swung on it. It seemed that there must have been a reason for it. Amelia was sure she had never written any of her stories down before that day. It was as if swinging on the lamp, and almost falling to her death, was the thing that had made her start. And yet if she had opened the door, she felt, none of the stories that she wrote would ever have taken shape. It was as if the lamp contained the stories – not only the ones about itself, but all the other ones that came into Amelia's mind – and Amelia only had to look at it to delve into the endless store of ideas that were locked up

38

inside it. But if she had managed to open the door that day, all the ideas would have flown away.

It would sound ridiculous to anyone else if she had to explain it, she knew, but to Amelia it seemed that somehow the lamp was deeply connected to the fact that she loved to write, or maybe was even responsible for it, and if the lamp was ever taken away from her, she imagined that she might never write another story again.

But Amelia didn't imagine that the most amazing stories don't necessarily start in a faraway palace, like the ones she made up about the lamp – or that if they do, they don't necessarily end there. She didn't suspect that the most extraordinary tales can end up in the most ordinary places, where you'd least expect them. Like Mr Vishwanath's studio on the ground floor of the green house that Solomon Weiszacker built. Or that they can come into your life without you even realising that it's happening, in the shape of something you've seen hundreds of times before, like a big cream-coloured car, for instance, coming down the street.

CHAPTER 5

Amelia saw the car from her window. It moved slowly along the street towards her. As it drew near to the green house the car veered gently towards the kerb, like a big stately ship coming into port, and then it came to a stop, directly in front of the sheet-covered window on the ground floor.

Amelia put down the book she had been reading and looked at the pavement below her. She knew what was about to happen next. It was always the same. Out of the front seat would get the driver, a small man in a blue suit. He would put a blue cap carefully on his head, and then he would go around the car to the passenger door and open it, and out would get the old lady, wearing a long fur coat that came right down to her ankles, whatever the weather.

The man went around the car and opened the door for the lady.

'Now he'll have to run after her,' murmured Amelia to the sculpted lady with the coffee and the coral outside her window. When the old lady got out of the car, she never said a word to the driver, but always walked straight past him, and the man would close the car door and run so he could get to the door of Mr Vishwanath's studio and open it before she got there. 'See?' murmured Amelia, as the driver scurried to the door.

The lady went inside. The man went back to the car, took off his cap, got back into the driver's seat, closed the door and waited. He would wait there like that, Amelia knew, for an hour. Then he would get out, put on his cap, walk around the car, open the passenger door and stand beside it, and invariably, a minute or so later, the old lady would come out of the green house, walk past him without a word and get into the car again.

From this height, the cream-coloured car looked very grand. But Amelia had seen it up close, on the street. It was old, the paintwork had lost its gleam, and the leather of the seats was cracked. The driver's uniform, which looked so smart from a distance, was worn and frayed, and the stitching on his cap was coming loose. The man himself was old and hunched, with thinning silver hair, and looked as if he should have retired long ago. Amelia felt sorry for him. He would sit in the car, without saying a word or even seeming to look at anything in particular, as people went past him. Even if a bunch of kids jumped around outside his window and made faces at him, as they sometimes did, he didn't respond, didn't do anything, until it was time to get out and open the door for the lady again.

41

Amelia had seen the old lady up close as well, a few times, when she happened to be outside as the old lady was arriving or leaving. The old lady was tall, quite thin, with knobbly fingers and lots of rings. Amelia wondered whether the lady could get the rings off over the knobbles in her fingers, and if not, how long the rings had been there. The lady's hair, which was pulled tightly back, was almost white, but her eyebrows were black. And she always had a very severe, hawk-like expression on her face, and she always looked straight ahead, as if nothing to either side of her was worthy of attention, not even her driver as he opened the car door. In short, Amelia didn't think she looked like a particularly nice person, and she wondered why Mr Vishwanath, who seemed to be so picky about his yoga students, wanted to teach her.

Assuming she really was a yoga student, of course.

Amelia knew that all the rumours about Mr Vishwanath being a spy or a crime boss were nonsense, so she knew the rumours about the lady being his accomplice were nonsense as well. But Amelia found it hard to believe the lady came to learn yoga. Once she had asked Mr Vishwanath what the lady really did when she came to his studio, but he hadn't said anything, or even acknowledged her question. Yet the lady looked too old for yoga, and she always came in a fur coat, which was the last thing she would have needed. And her expression was always so harsh, with none of the peace, none of the contentment, that showed so strongly in Mr Vishwanath's face. Maybe she was an old friend of Mr Vishwanath, or a relative, and went there to visit him. If so, Amelia didn't think much of her. She didn't think much of the way the old lady left the small man sitting in the car when she went inside. She was probably having tea and cake with Mr Vishwanath, enjoying herself, while the man in the car had nothing. And she never brought anything out to him. That was another thing that made Amelia dislike her.

'What do you think she's doing in there?' murmured Amelia, still gazing at the street, although a couple of minutes must have passed since the old lady had disappeared into Mr Vishwanath's studio and the driver had gone back to the car. She gazed for a moment longer, then glanced at the sculpted lady outside her window, who stared down with her sightless eyes.

Amelia went back to reading. It was a horror story she had just started about a killer hamster that gets caught in an X-ray machine in a laboratory and grows to the size of a wolf, but because Amelia had read so many horror stories she could quickly tell which ones were any good. This one wasn't particularly promising, which was why she had been looking out the window and saw the cream-coloured car coming down Marburg Street in the first place.

The sound of banging and chiselling came from the sculpture room. Painting and weaving were much quieter arts, and Amelia often wished her mother would spend more of her time on them. Lately, she had spent all her time in the sculpture room, and wouldn't let anyone in to see what she was doing. Amelia's father said that probably indicated the start of a new phase. What made Amelia's mother go from one phase to the next was a mystery to Amelia. Still, it was probably a good thing if it meant there weren't going to be any more of the narrow so-called faces in the garden. On the other hand, it might not be such a good thing if something even worse appeared.

The intercom on Amelia's wall buzzed. It was a system her father had invented, with a number of improvements which supposedly made it superior to every other intercom system in the world. Or would, when he had perfected them. The fact that it wasn't quite finished hadn't stopped him installing it.

'Amelia, can you . . . I need . . . come . . . and bring . . . quickly because . . .'

Amelia sighed. That was better than usual. Even hearing the buzz of the intercom was better than usual.

She waited, still listening. A few more words came out, then there was a kind of scrunchy crackling. Then silence.

44

Her father would be in his invention shed in the garden. Amelia put the book aside and left her room. On the second floor, the banging behind the door to the sculpture room was loud. Amelia went all the way down. Mrs Ellis was beating eggs in the kitchen as she went past.

The door to Mr Vishwanath's studio was open. Amelia stopped. She knew that at that very moment the old lady was inside.

Amelia hesitated. Mr Vishwanath's door wasn't normally open. He must have forgotten to close it properly when the old lady arrived. Amelia had never actually been inside the studio. The door opened into a small kitchen, and from the kitchen a passageway led further in. You could see that much from the back door. But where the passageway went, Amelia didn't know.

She knew she shouldn't go in. Mr Vishwanath valued his privacy. But Amelia was dying to find out what the old lady was doing in there. Maybe it was because this would finally give her the chance to disprove all the rumours that Eugenie and Kevin and everyone else were always spreading. Or maybe it was Amelia's dislike of the old lady that made her curiosity so intense. What could such a severe, ungenerous old woman possibly be doing with Mr Vishwanath, who was such a good, gentle man?

The kitchen was small and simple. Almost at once, Amelia was at the passageway on the other side.

The passageway was unlit. It led past another small room which had no window and was dark inside. Amelia glanced in. She caught the scent of the oil Mr Vishwanath rubbed on himself before he started his yoga exercises. She could make out a kind of mat on the floor. It looked like the room where Mr Vishwanath slept. Amelia was feeling guiltier and guiltier. At the end of the passageway, a door stood slightly ajar, and light came through the crack.

Amelia went to it. She stood behind the door and listened.

Silence.

Amelia put her eye to the crack. All she could see was a blank strip of wall.

She pushed the door. Then a little further. She put her head around it.

Light. The room was big, open, airy. On the opposite side was the sheet over the front window, with a soft, even light coming through it. In the middle of the room stood Mr Vishwanath, his back towards Amelia, in his blue yoga nappy. The old lady was facing him, wearing a green leotard. Both of them were standing on one foot with their other foot around their neck. The old lady's eyes were closed.

Amelia stared. The expression on the old lady's face

was calm, even gentle. The harshness had gone. It was more like Mr Vishwanath's expression, suffused with a kind of peace and contentment.

Mr Vishwanath murmured something. The woman opened her eyes.

She saw Amelia. In an instant, her face changed, as if the calm, gentle expression had been nothing but a mask.

'How *dare* you!' cried the lady.

It was another moment before Mr Vishwanath could get his foot off his neck and look around.

By then Amelia had fled.

CHAPTER 6

Amelia didn't stop until she was back in her room and the door was closed behind her.

She was panting for breath. She peered out the window, hiding behind the edge of the curtain. The old lady was marching out of Mr Vishwanath's studio. The driver wasn't ready for her, and Amelia saw him jump out, hastily slapping his hat on his head as he scurried around the car. The old lady waited as the man fumbled at the door. For a moment, Amelia forgot about what she herself had done and watched the lady on the street below in distaste. Was the old lady too good even to open a simple car door for herself?

Then the lady got in, the man went back to the driver's seat, and the big cream-coloured car pulled out and moved off down the street. And Amelia was left thinking about what she had done, the shame and dishonesty of it. How she had crept into Mr Vishwanath's home. Like a sneak. Like a thief.

She opened her door a fraction and listened to the sounds coming from the house. There was a banging in the sculpture room. Between the bangs, nothing.

Amelia continued to listen, trying to hear if anyone was coming up the stairs.

She closed the door and sat down on her bed. She didn't know what was going to happen next. Maybe Mr Vishwanath was waiting to see one of her parents and tell them about it.

She listened. Still nothing.

The minutes passed. Amelia almost wished she could hear someone coming up the stairs. Shame and guilt kept building up in her.

Eventually Amelia came out of her room.

She waited for a moment, listening, looking down over the banister under the lamp. Then she went slowly back down the stairs, past Mrs Ellis in the kitchen, who was busy chopping something and hadn't noticed her run past before and looked up too late to see her go by now.

She found Mr Vishwanath sitting on his chair outside the back door in his faded red shirt and old brown trousers.

Amelia hesitated, still standing. Mr Vishwanath didn't say anything. Didn't look at her.

Amelia sat down beside him.

The minutes passed. Slowly. Awkwardly. Amelia kept glancing at Mr Vishwanath. She wished he would say something. But he just kept gazing at the garden.

'I'm sorry, Mr Vishwanath,' said Amelia at last.

Mr Vishwanath didn't speak.

Amelia waited. Then she said it again. 'I'm sorry, Mr Vishwanath. I really am. I don't know what came over me. It's just the door was open and . . . well, I just wanted to see. I asked you before what the old lady did when she came to you, and you wouldn't say, so I . . . I . . .' Amelia stopped. That was no excuse. 'I'm sorry. That's all I can say, Mr Vishwanath. I'm really, really sorry. I know I shouldn't have done what I did. How can I make it up to you?'

Now, at last, Mr Vishwanath looked at her. 'To me?' he said, in his soft voice, like the gentle thrumming of a drum. 'Do you think you have injured me?'

Amelia frowned.

'It's not me you have injured, Amelia. It's not me you have to make it up to.'

Who was it? A horrible thought crossed Amelia's mind. Not the old lady! She didn't want to make anything up to *her*.

But it wasn't the old lady. Suddenly Amelia understood. Something in the way Mr Vishwanath was watching her made it clear. It wasn't himself he was talking about, and it wasn't the old lady either.

'The things we do that we wish we have not done, the one we injure most is ourself,' said Mr Vishwanath.

Amelia frowned. She wasn't sure about that. 'What if you kill someone?'

'You kill yourself as well. The other person dies physically, but you yourself die in a different way.'

'But at least you're not dead!'

'True,' said Mr Vishwanath, but he said it in such a tone that Amelia knew he meant it was true in one way, but not in another.

Amelia thought about it. Mr Vishwanath was right. Stealing into his studio like that hadn't really hurt Mr Vishwanath. But it had left her with a sense of guilt and shame that almost made her hate herself. All she wanted now was a chance to prove herself again.

'Mr Vishwanath, have you ever done things you wished you hadn't?'

Mr Vishwanath didn't answer. After a moment there was a slight smile on his lips.

Of course not, thought Amelia. Stupid question. He had never done anything bad, not Mr Vishwanath.

'In my youth,' he murmured, 'I was quite a terror.'

Amelia looked at him doubtfully. A terror? Mr Vishwanath?

The smile lingered a moment longer, then was gone. Mr Vishwanath's expression was perfectly serious again. 'Every day it is a new battle, to do what we should. And if we have been successful yesterday, it doesn't mean that the battle today is going to be any less hard.'

'But you hardly ever go out of your house, Mr Vishwanath! How hard can it be for you?'

Mr Vishwanath nodded. Amelia didn't know exactly what that meant.

They sat in silence, staring at the sculptures in the garden.

'So you're not angry with me?' asked Amelia eventually.

'Only as angry as you are with yourself,' said Mr Vishwanath.

Amelia frowned. 'I bet the old lady was angry!'

Mr Vishwanath didn't reply.

'I bet she's angry with everybody! She looks so sour. And do you see what she does to that man who drives the car for her? She's so mean! She makes him sit there all the time that . . .'

Amelia stopped. Mr Vishwanath was looking at her.

'Why do you teach her, Mr Vishwanath?' Amelia thought of the stories about the people Mr Vishwanath refused to teach, and yet he was happy to teach yoga to such an unpleasant person. 'Does she pay you a lot?'

'She pays me if she has the money,' replied Mr Vishwanath.

'You mean sometimes she *doesn't* pay you?'

'Money is not the most important thing.'

'You mean she comes and she doesn't pay you? She has that big car and—'

'She is a very old student of mine,' said Mr Vishwanath. 'She has been coming to me for many years.'

'But she's so horrible!'

'Have you ever even spoken to her, Amelia?'

'But you can see it!'

Mr Vishwanath sighed. 'In every person, Amelia, there is a beauty.'

Amelia started to laugh.

'You cannot tell from the outside.'

Mr Vishwanath's voice was soft, almost too soft to hear. Amelia stopped laughing. She remembered the look on the old lady's face in Mr Vishwanath's studio, in that split second before the lady opened her eyes and saw Amelia spying on her. Calm. Gentle. Beautiful?

'Is she angry with you now?' asked Amelia quietly. 'Because of me?'

Mr Vishwanath didn't reply.

'Is she not going to come back, Mr Vishwanath?'

Mr Vishwanath was silent for a moment. 'She is easily angered. That is one of her faults.'

'Why?'

'In her own way, she has had a hard life. Yet most people would think it has been easy. Materially. The easier others think it, the harder it seems to her.'

'Mr Vishwanath, that sounds like a riddle.'

'Look,' said Mr Vishwanath. 'Here comes your father.'

Amelia jumped. For a second, she thought Mr

Vishwanath was going to tell her father about what she had done. Then she knew that was the last thing he would do.

Her father wandered absentmindedly towards them from the shed at the end of the garden, staring at the ground as he made his way through the sculptures. He didn't notice Mr Vishwanath and Amelia until he had almost reached the verandah.

'Oh,' he said. 'Hello.'

Amelia smiled.

'Hello,' said Mr Vishwanath.

Amelia's father frowned. 'Didn't I . . . Amelia, didn't I call you before?'

'When?'

'On the intercom. Didn't I call you?'

'Why would you have called me?'

'I needed something. That's right. I remember now, I needed something urgently.'

'What was it?' asked Amelia.

Amelia's father frowned again. 'I don't know . . . I must have . . . Amelia, if I need something urgently, you have to bring it. Do you understand? If I don't have it, I may as well not even bother!'

'Alright,' said Amelia.

'If no one ever got things when they needed them, no one would manage to invent anything new. And you know what would happen then, don't you?'

54

'We'd still be in the Stone Age,' said Amelia under her breath.

'We'd still be in the Stone Age!' said Amelia's father. Amelia nodded.

Amelia's father frowned again. 'What was it that I needed?' he muttered to himself, and rubbed his chin. 'What *was* it?' He turned around and began to walk back to the shed, still frowning and muttering, having forgotten about whatever it was that had made him come out of the shed in the first place.

Amelia watched him. She wondered what it would be like to have a father like other children had. Or at least one who wasn't exactly like the one she had.

Eventually she shrugged. She turned back to Mr Vishwanath.

'Mr Vishwanath, if that old lady's life is so hard, she should do something to make it easier. No point complaining about it.'

'Many people would say her life has not been hard.'

'Then even less point!' exclaimed Amelia.

'Maybe it isn't so simple,' said Mr Vishwanath.

'And maybe it isn't so complicated,' replied Amelia, although she had no idea now what Mr Vishwanath was talking about, and she just said it because it sounded right. Although why should it be so complicated? Why should anything be complicated, if you just took the time to think about it sensibly?

Mr Vishwanath was watching her as if something was going through his mind. Something he wasn't sure about.

'What is it, Mr Vishwanath?' asked Amelia.

Mr Vishwanath thought for a moment longer. 'Would you like to meet her?' he said at last. 'The old lady, as you call her?'

'Not particularly,' said Amelia.

'Are you scared to?'

'No. Who is she?'

'The Princess Parvin Kha-Douri.'

CHAPTER 7

The thought of meeting the old lady really was a bit scary, even though Amelia had told Mr Vishwanath that it wasn't. But the thought of meeting a princess was exciting. And no one could have been more excited than Eugenie, even though she wasn't even going to meet her.

'A princess!' she said, for about the fiftieth time.

'I know,' said Amelia, for the forty-ninth.

'A real princess!'

'Eugenie, I think we're all aware of that now,' said Kevin.

They were walking home after a hockey game, carrying their sticks.

'You'll have to curtsy, Amelia,' said Eugenie suddenly. 'Properly. I'll show you how.'

Eugenie dropped right there on the footpath, flinging out her arms and almost hitting Kevin with her stick. It was a low, extravagant curtsy, head bent, nose only a couple of centimetres from the pavement.

Eugenie glanced up at Amelia. 'Now you do it.'

'Eugenie, I know how to curtsy.'

'Show me.'

'Eugenie, I *know*.'

Eugenie looked at her doubtfully. Then she straightened up. 'Well, you've seen now, anyway,' she said rather pompously. 'You can practise at home.'

They started walking again.

'She's too old to be a princess,' said Kevin.

'What's that supposed to mean?' demanded Eugenie.

'Princesses are meant to be young.'

'And then they get old.'

'Then they're meant to be queens.'

'Only if they marry a prince, or if they're heir to the throne. But they're always a princess. No one can take that away from them.' Eugenie sighed. 'A princess . . . Princess Parvin Kha-Douri.' She murmured the name softly, as it was almost too precious to say out loud.

'Well, it seems ridiculous to me,' muttered Kevin, 'still being a princess when you're that old.'

Eugenie didn't reply to that. She stuck her nose in the air.

They stopped at the Sticky Sunday ice-cream shop. Kevin got a double scoop of Caramel and Hazelnut. Amelia got Raspberry Ripple and Walnuts 'n' Cream. Eugenie spent a long time examining all the possibilities and got a small serve of frozen yoghurt. They sat down on the stools along the wall.

'If you don't want to see her, Amelia,' said Eugenie, 'I'll go instead.'

'Mr Vishwanath didn't invite you,' said Kevin.

'I'm sure he wouldn't mind.'

'He invited Amelia.'

'And she doesn't know whether she wants to go.'

'Of course I want to go,' said Amelia. 'It's just . . .'

Eugenie and Kevin watched her expectantly.

'What?'

Amelia didn't say. She had told Eugenie and Kevin that Mr Vishwanath had invited her to meet the Princess – not what she had done half an hour before he made the suggestion.

Eugenie watched her for a moment longer. Then she leaned forward earnestly. 'You must go, Amelia. A princess! It's a once-in-a-lifetime opportunity. You'll never forgive yourself if you don't.'

Kevin shook his head. 'Don't go if you don't want to.'

'Kevin!' Eugenie almost shrieked.

'What difference does it make if she's a princess? I bet she thinks she's terribly important, but just being a princess doesn't make her more important than anyone else.'

'Of course it makes her more important than anyone else!'

'Why? Just because she's the daughter of a king? Just because she was born into a particular family?'

Eugenie shook her head impatiently. Then she glanced at Amelia, and shook it again, as if to ask what you could do with a person who said things like that.

Amelia frowned. Perhaps Kevin was right. The fact that a person was born into a particular family shouldn't make her important. On the other hand, perhaps Eugenie was right. You could meet plenty of people who thought they were important any day, but you couldn't just go out and meet a princess, who really might be.

Besides, it wasn't because the Princess was important – or considered herself to be important – that Amelia thought it would be interesting to meet her, but to hear about her life. That would have to be interesting. Although she was so stern, and so forbidding, and Amelia hadn't exactly got off to the best start with her.

Amelia licked her ice-cream thoughtfully. She watched the lady serving behind the counter. Her name was Mrs Egmont and she always went about her work very seriously. Her husband, Mr Egmont, was a much more cheerful character, and always gave you more ice-cream than you paid for.

Mrs Egmont was serving up a triple-scooper, and a little boy, who looked barely big enough to manage a double-scooper, was waiting greedily for it. He had his money ready in his grubby little hands, and was jumping from foot to foot in excitement.

Suddenly Amelia was aware of silence around her. She looked back at Kevin and Eugenie.

'Well?' said Kevin. 'Are you going to meet her, or aren't you?'

Amelia shrugged. 'Mr Vishwanath said he'll introduce me next Saturday, if I want.'

'Oh, Amelia . . .' said Eugenie. She sighed. 'Next Saturday! You're so lucky. You must, you really must. It's a once-in-a-lifetime opportunity. To meet a princess. A real princess. How glamorous!'

Eugenie's eyes were sparkling with excitement. But Eugenie hadn't seen the Princess as Amelia had seen her, wearing a green leotard and standing on one foot with the other foot hooked around her neck. Even Eugenie might have found it hard to think about the Princess as someone glamorous if she had seen her like that.

'Do you have to wear anything special?' asked Eugenie.

'No,' said Amelia.

'I could lend you my pink top,' said Eugenie. 'The one with the lace.'

'I don't need it.'

'Princesses like lace.'

'How do you know?' asked Kevin.

'Because I do. They like sewing, as well.'

'Sewing?' demanded Kevin incredulously.

'Yes. All princesses are taught to sew.'

'Why would they need to? They can buy whatever they want.'

'They don't *need* to. That's exactly the point. It's *because* they don't need to. A princess can learn to do anything. They can play the piano and do watercolours and speak all kinds of languages.'

'Did you hear that, Amelia?' said Kevin. 'A princess can learn to do anything, and the less she needs to do, the more she wants to do it. Alright, Eugenie. What else can you tell us about princesses?'

A lot of things, apparently. The list was almost endless. As they left the Sticky Sunday, Eugenie was still telling them. The fact that Eugenie had the same name as a long-dead French empress seemed to give her some special kind of closeness to royalty, at least in her own mind. She was so excited about the prospect of Amelia meeting the Princess that it almost made Amelia decide not to go, just to see what Eugenie would do. But it really was a once-in-a-lifetime opportunity, as Eugenie had said. Or at least a once-until-now-in-her-lifetime opportunity, because Amelia couldn't tell what other opportunities would come along in her lifetime, possibly including the chance to meet another princess. But possibly not. So possibly it was a once-in-a-lifetime opportunity. And Amelia wasn't the kind of person to give up a once-in-a-lifetime opportunity, or even an opportunity that might only possibly be one.

Although the Princess was definitely scary. But she couldn't be as horrible as she seemed, thought Amelia. No one could. She must really be a very nice old lady. That was what Mr Vishwanath had said, wasn't it? She was probably very pleasant once you started talking to her. Even to someone who had crept in and spied on her in her leotard. Of course she would be. It would be very interesting to meet her, and definitely not an opportunity to be missed, and the Princess would be very nice, Amelia told herself. And she would almost have believed it, if not for the feeling of anxiety that kept gnawing at her stomach.

'Of course, you'll have to bring her a gift,' said Eugenie.

Kevin stared at her. He stopped right there on the pavement, hockey stick over his shoulder, staring, as if this was the most preposterous thing he had heard from Eugenie yet. 'What are you talking about? Why does she need a gift? She's a princess. She has everything already.'

'Doesn't matter,' said Eugenie. She turned to Amelia. 'Amelia, you *must* take a gift. Everyone must when they meet a princess. It shows respect. Nothing could be ruder than to turn up without one.'

Kevin glanced doubtfully at Amelia.

'How do you know?' asked Amelia.

Eugenie put her nose in the air. 'Go without a gift if

you don't believe me. Just see what happens. Go on. Just go without one.'

Amelia frowned. There was no reason to suppose that Eugenie knew anything at all about princesses, including whether you had to have a gift when you met one. But there was something about the idea that appealed to Amelia. If she could think of a special gift, that was. Something memorable. Something that would show the Princess that even if she really was as important as she thought she was, and even if there were all kinds of things she had learned to do, Amelia herself wasn't without talent, either.

'I bet I know what Martin Martinez would take!' said Kevin, and he grinned.

Eugenie laughed at that, forgetting that her nose was meant to be in the air.

'Something featuring a certain boy . . .' said Kevin.

'From Argentina!' added Eugenie, and they both laughed so much they almost dropped their hockey sticks.

Amelia forced herself to smile. But only for a moment. Kevin and Eugenie continued to make fun of Martin Martinez and the latest story he had put in the school magazine. It was about a boy who had written a story and won an international prize and was asked by the President of Argentina to write a national story, which was something like a national anthem, only in the form of a story. It wasn't hard to guess who the main character was based on.

It was a terrible story, and everyone thought so. It got into the school magazine only because no one else had submitted anything. Amelia could have submitted any number of stories that were better. She had two drawers full, and then there were the stories about the peacock lamp. They weren't written down, but were all in her head, as if they were the most special, the most precious, and only for a particularly important occasion would she actually put one of them in writing. But even the ones in the drawers, any one of them, would have been better than Martin's rubbish story about the boy who won the international prize from the President of Argentina.

But at least Martin had submitted it, thought Amelia. At least he didn't just leave it in a drawer somewhere after he had written it, even if everyone would have been better off if that was exactly where it had stayed.

At least, when the occasion presented itself, he was prepared to show what he could do.

CHAPTER 8

Amelia watched the cream-coloured car come slowly down the street. It pulled up below her, as it always did, in front of Mr Vishwanath's studio. Out stepped the driver in his blue suit. He put on his hat and went around the car. Out came the old lady, dressed in her fur coat, and swept past him, and he hurried to get to the door before her.

Then he went back to the car, took off his hat, and got in again.

Mr Vishwanath had told Amelia that she had to wait for an hour after she saw the Princess arrive. Only then, after the Princess had done her yoga, would they be ready for her.

Another hour! Amelia didn't know if the time was too long or too short.

She tried to read. She had finished the killer hamster story and was halfway through a new book, a crime story. But Amelia had worked out who the murderer was after about two chapters, and she hadn't been able to resist checking the end of the book to see whether she was right – which she was – so there wasn't much point continuing, even if she had been able to concentrate. Which she couldn't, not this morning, anyway. She read the same page about five times and kept having to go back to the start.

Amelia looked down. The car stood by the kerb. She glanced at the carved, eyeless lady that Solomon Wieszacker had put at the top of the house. A pigeon was perched on her head. The pigeon gazed at Amelia, and then cocked its head, as pigeons do, still gazing at her. There were some crumbs on Amelia's desk from a biscuit she had eaten. She picked up the crumbs and put them out on the window ledge and took a step back. The pigeon looked at the crumbs, then at Amelia, then at the crumbs, and suddenly flapped across. It gobbled them quickly and flew off.

Banging came from the sculpture room. Amelia's mother had hardly come out for days now, which was a sure sign that a new phase was starting, and she was extremely short-tempered when she did come out, which was an even surer one. But it could take weeks, sometimes months, of trial and error when a new phase was starting, before Amelia's mother actually worked out what the sculptures of the phase were going to be. And in that time there was inevitably an awful lot of banging, and shouting, and even smashing inside the sculpture room.

Amelia listened to the banging. Suddenly she felt as

if she couldn't spend even another minute waiting up here. She'd burst!

In the kitchen, Mrs Ellis was stirring a pot. She looked up and saw Amelia standing in the doorway.

'What are you up to now?' said Mrs Ellis.

'Nothing,' replied Amelia.

Mrs Ellis looked as if she didn't quite believe her. 'What are those pages you're holding?'

Amelia put her hand behind her back. 'Nothing,' she said.

Mrs Ellis raised an eyebrow. She dipped a little finger in the pot and tasted it quickly. Then she added more salt. 'Nothing means something,' she muttered to herself. 'That's what I always say, young lady.' She looked up to see what Amelia would reply to that, but the doorway was empty.

Outside, Amelia sat on the chair near the back door of Mr Vishwanath's studio. She looked at the thin white sculptures in the grass. They would have to be moved soon if her mother was starting a new phase. Her father would stack them down the back of the garden with the globular sculptures and the angular sculptures and the twisted sculptures and the other sculptures from all of her mother's previous phases. He had invented a statue-moving-and-stacking machine especially for the purpose, which looked like a small trolley on wheels with a little winch to lift each statue on and off. He was very proud of this invention, which was one of the few that did what it was supposed to do. At least most of the time.

One day, thought Amelia, there wouldn't be room down the back of the garden to stack all the old sculptures. Not if her mother kept going from one phase into another so frequently and refused to let any of them be taken out of the garden.

Amelia thought about what she was going to say to the Princess. The awful anxiety she felt when she imagined actually facing up to the old lady hadn't gone away, and she had tried not to think about it. Now that the moment was so close, she almost wanted to run away and hide. She tried to imagine what she would say at the start. She could just say hello. That seemed a bit bare. Eugenie had said she would have to say *Your Highness*. After every sentence. 'Hello, Your Highness.' Maybe she would start with 'Good Morning, Your Highness'. That's what Eugenie would say, probably, and she would do one of her flamboyant curtsies. Or five. Amelia didn't know if she wanted to curtsy. She had thought about that and she couldn't decide. Maybe she should bow. But she didn't know whether she wanted to bow, either.

And what was she going to say then? Something about being sorry for spying on the Princess in Mr Vishwanath's studio. *Your Highness*. And what would the old lady say to that? Amelia didn't even want to think about it. It would be a lot easier if she really did run away and hide. There was still time.

Amelia saw her father come out of the shed at the bottom of the garden. He was almost at the verandah before he noticed her.

'Hello,' he said. 'How long have you been sitting there?'

'Twelve minutes,' said Amelia, although she didn't really know, and it could have been thirteen minutes, or eleven. Or eight, for that matter, or sixteen.

'Didn't hear an explosion, did you?' said her father.

'Where?' asked Amelia.

'Down there.' Her father pointed to the shed.

Amelia shook her head.

'No, neither did I.' Her father frowned. 'Odd. I was expecting one.'

He crossed his arms, and gazed thoughtfully at the shed.

Suddenly there was a loud pop. Purple smoke poured out of the shed's windows.

Amelia's father beamed. 'There we are! Perfect!'

They both watched the shed. Eventually the smoke stopped coming out of the windows. Only a few purple wisps hung around the roof.

From the sculpture room above them, they heard a bang. And then a shout of frustration.

Amelia's father grinned. 'We'll have to move the sculptures soon. I've made improvements to the machine.'

'Oh,' said Amelia. 'It was working pretty well before.'

'Now it'll work better!'

Amelia looked at him doubtfully.

'You can't just stand on the spot, Amelia! You should never be satisfied. Things can always be improved. Remember that. If people didn't try to improve things, we'd still be in the Stone Age.'

'Yes,' said Amelia.

Her father nodded. Then he frowned slightly. 'Are you waiting for something?'

'Not really,' said Amelia.

'What have you been doing this morning? Reading?'

'Yes,' said Amelia. 'Kind of . . .'

'Always reading, Amelia.'

Amelia shrugged.

'What's that you're holding?'

'Nothing.' Amelia folded her arms, hiding the pages in her hand against her chest.

Her father didn't say anything.

'It's nothing.'

Her father looked at her questioningly for a moment longer. Then he nodded. 'Alright. Well, best be getting back, I suppose.'

'Yes,' said Amelia.

'There might be another explosion. Don't be concerned.'

'No,' said Amelia.

Her father headed back to the shed.

Amelia watched him go. He picked his way through the white sculptures, then stopped near one and looked at it. He cocked his head thoughtfully. An idea was going through his mind, Amelia could see. Probably about yet another improvement he could make to the statue-stacker. He was always having ideas, that was one of the things Amelia loved most about her father. Almost all of them were rubbish, which was one of the things she loved least. Although, in a funny way, she loved that as well.

He turned around and kept going, and a moment later the shed door closed behind him.

Amelia thought about the Princess again. It couldn't be much longer now. Her stomach knotted. After she had apologised, she didn't know what she was going to say to the Princess. Or what the Princess would say to her. She looked at the pages she was holding. It was one thing to have written them. She wondered if she really did have the courage to show them.

Maybe she should just get up and go while she still had the chance. Mr Vishwanath would understand.

'Amelia.'

Amelia jumped.

Mr Vishwanath was behind her. 'Amelia, the Princess is ready for you now.'

The Princess was sitting at a small table in a corner of Mr Vishwanath's yoga room, draped in her fur coat. She was staring at the sheet-covered window, and made no movement to show that she knew anyone was there. Amelia stopped. Whatever she had thought about saying, and doing, went out of her mind.

'Go on, Amelia,' murmured Mr Vishwanath.

Amelia went closer. Finally the Princess looked around.

'Hello,' said Amelia.

The Princess's eyes narrowed. Her dark eyebrows contracted slightly. That was all.

'Sit down, Amelia,' whispered Mr Vishwanath.

Amelia hesitated for a moment, then sat down at the table opposite the Princess. The Princess continued to watch her with a sharp, hawk-like gaze, as if measuring her, as if Amelia was some kind of species of creature unlike the Princess herself, and liable to act in the most unpredictable fashion.

'You are Amelia,' said the Princess at last. Her voice was low, and she had an accent that Amelia couldn't identify. When she said her name, she said 'Ehmeeelieh'.

Amelia nodded.

'I am the Princess Parvin Kha-Douri,' said the Princess. 'You may not say my name when you speak to me. You must say "Your Serenity".'

Not *Your Highness*. So much for Eugenie and her supposed royal expertise, thought Amelia.

'Only someone of my rank or above may say my name.'

'What does that mean?' asked Amelia. 'Someone of your rank or above?'

'Someone who is a princess or more than a princess,' replied the Princess stiffly.

Amelia glanced at Mr Vishwanath.

'The maestro may say my name,' said the Princess. 'He is my teacher. That is a kind of rank. An honorary rank. You are not my teacher, I think!'

Amelia shook her head.

'No,' said the Princess coldly. 'I do not think so.'

Amelia glanced at Mr Vishwanath again. He nodded reassuringly. Then he sat on the floor and adopted one of his yoga poses, legs crossed, arms outstretched, wrists turned upwards, as if the conversation between Amelia and the Princess was a matter for them alone, and none of his business. He closed his eyes. Already, Amelia could see, his mind was far away from what was happening in this room.

'I do not normally meet children,' said the Princess.

Amelia looked back at her.

'It was only because the maestro requested it. Normally, I would not meet a child such as you.'

Amelia glanced at Mr Vishwanath. There was nothing on his face – not a flicker, not a glance – to show that he had heard.

'Do you know why?' said the Princess.

Amelia silently shook her head.

'Because children behave disgracefully. Last time, you behaved disgracefully. I suppose now you wish to apologise to me for this.'

'Yes,' said Amelia. 'I shouldn't have done that.'

'What?'

'What I did.'

'Is that an apology?'

'Yes.'

'Then say sorry,' said the Princess. 'In an apology, in your language, one must say sorry, I think. Otherwise it is not a proper apology.'

'Sorry,' said Amelia.

The Princess continued to stare at her, one black eyebrow raised expectantly.

'Your Serenity,' mumbled Amelia.

'Good,' said the Princess. But there was no warmth

or pleasure or satisfaction in the way she had said it. Her gaze was as stern as before.

There was silence.

Amelia had the feeling the Princess didn't care about her at all, didn't want to know anything about her, had absolutely no interest in her. All she cared about was receiving an apology, a 'proper' apology, and that wasn't because she cared about Amelia, but because she cared about herself. About her rank. About how important she was.

'What is that you are holding?' asked the Princess.

Amelia glanced at the pages in her hand. They were getting crumpled, she was gripping them so tight.

'Well?'

'It's just . . . It doesn't matter,' muttered Amelia.

'What? What is it?'

Amelia frowned. 'It's a story.'

'Did you write it?' said the Princess. 'For me?'

Amelia wished she had never brought the pages with her. She wished she had never even written them. Mr Vishwanath was wrong, there wasn't anything nice about the old lady, there was no beauty within her. She was harsh, horrible. Amelia didn't want to show her the story she had written. Suddenly the story seemed like a soft, fragile little creature, and if she showed it to her, the old lady with her angry gaze and her haughty tone was just going to stomp all over it.

'Well?' said the Princess.

Reluctantly, almost trembling, Amelia held out the crumpled pages.

But the Princess made no movement to take them. 'Read it to me.'

Amelia stared.

'Read,' said the Princess, and then she looked away at the sheet-covered window again, and gave a little sigh, as if she didn't really care about Amelia's story, except in the sense that it was something that had been done because she was a princess, and since people always want to do things for a princess, a princess is obliged to pretend that she's interested. But not too interested. In fact, rather bored.

Amelia hesitated. But the Princess remained impassive, waiting for her to commence.

Amelia looked down at the first page. 'There was a princess once . . .'

'Louder,' said the Princess. 'I can't hear you. If you want to read the story you wrote for me, speak so I can hear you.'

Amelia took a deep breath. 'There was a princess once . . .' she began again, more loudly. 'She lived in a palace with all kinds of marvellous things, gold and jewels and beautiful clothes and lovely furniture, but the thing she loved most was the lamp in her room. They didn't have electricity in those days, so they had to light oil in the lamp each day and put it out each night. The lamp was made of bronze, and it had six sides and a top and a bottom, and the metalwork of the lamp was very rich, with all kinds of rare and wonderful animals carved in it with such skill and such cleverness you could barely see them unless you looked very closely. There was a tiger, and an eagle, and a rhinoceros, and monkeys chasing each other around the light and one of them had the face of a person. And the bottom of the lamp was made up of a pair of magnificent peacocks. To light the lamp, there was a little door . . .'

Amelia read. She gazed strictly at the page, concentrated wholly on the words, as if by doing that, and forgetting about the Princess, she could protect her story from the withering harshness of the lady who sat opposite her. So she didn't see the Princess turn her head as she spoke. She didn't see the look on the Princess's face as she described the lamp. She didn't see the Princess's hand go to her mouth, and her eyes go wide, nor hear her stifled gasp at the mention of the monkey with the face of the man, or her second gasp at the mention of the two peacocks on the bottom of the lamp. And she didn't see the way the Princess looked at her after that, without any hint of practised boredom, but with a kind of stunned disbelief.

Amelia didn't see any of that. And after a while she did forget about the Princess, losing herself in the words she had written, the images she had created, the flow of the story of the princess and the lamp, how the princess would light the lamp each night, and how it wasn't lit when she was kept away from the man she loved, and how they were reunited at the end and the lamp came alight for one last night. It wasn't one of the bloodcurdling versions, with the ghost of the princess and phantom beasts coming to life and lots of blood everywhere, but it wasn't the soppiest version either. It was the one, in truth, that was Amelia's own favourite.

When she was finished, she put the pages down, and only then did she remember where she was, and why she was reading it, and who she was reading it to.

The Princess didn't say anything. She was staring at Amelia blankly, as if not seeing her at all.

'That's it,' whispered Amelia.

The Princess gave a little jerk. Her expression became severe again, impatient, dismissive.

'Hm! It is a silly story. A fancy!' She said the word contemptuously, in her heavy accent. A *fenceeee*.

Amelia winced.

'Life is not like this. Why did you write such a story?'

'I just thought . . . I thought you'd like it.'

'It is a stupid story. Stupid! Do you hear me?'

Amelia stared. It was the first story she had ever written – apart from the ones she was forced to write at school – that she had showed to anyone. And it wasn't just any story, it was about the lamp – the lamp which had almost killed her, yet had also saved her life, the lamp about which she knew so little, and yet contained so many stories – and of all these stories, it was the one she loved most. For years, she had carried it in her head, thinking about it, developing it, perfecting it. It was the most precious story she had! And she had wasted it on this Princess. Amelia could feel tears coming to her eyes. But she wouldn't cry. Not here. Not in front of this awful, awful lady.

'Do you think this is what life is like to be a princess?' The Princess laughed bitterly. 'Do you think it is so simple? No, it is hard, harder than any other life.'

'Why?' said Amelia. 'Why is it so complicated? You have everything. You've got palaces, and people to look after you, and—'

'Stupid story! Why do you write about this lamp?'

Amelia shook her head, not sure what to say.

'Well? This lamp?' The Princess said it as if Amelia had no right even to mention it.

'It's just a lamp,' murmured Amelia.

'How do you know about it? With the monkey with the face of a man. With the peacocks on the bottom. The two peacocks. How do you know about the two peacocks? How do you know about this lamp?'

81

'I've seen it,' said Amelia.

The Princess stared. Now Amelia saw the Princess's face as it had been before, when Amelia had been reading. The old woman's eyes were full of amazement and disbelief.

'Where have you seen it?' asked the Princess.

'It's . . .'

'Where?' demanded the Princess. 'Where is it?'

'In my house,' whispered Amelia. 'Outside my room.'

The Princess stared at her again. Then her face flickered with a kind of tremor of horror. She turned away. She got up, holding her hand to the side of her face so Amelia couldn't see her expression, and went quickly to the door.

'I can't see the point of it,' said Amelia to Mr Vishwanath later, when they were sitting under the verandah. 'Why did you want me to meet her? She didn't care about anything I said. And then she just got up and walked out!'

Mr Vishwanath didn't respond. He continued to gaze at the garden, where Amelia's father was moving the statues of her mother's thin-white-faces phase down the back.

Or trying to. His improvements to the mover-and-stacker machine still needed some work. The winch was larger, which helped with the bigger statues, but that made the machine top-heavy, and it had developed a tendency to topple over when lifting the sculptures. It had already toppled over half a dozen times. But that didn't disturb Amelia's father, who knew that any improvement takes a number of attempts to get right. In fact, he would have been more disturbed had the machine not toppled over. Or at least that's what he claimed, calling out to them cheerfully as the machine toppled over on its side for the seventh time.

Mr Vishwanath smiled encouragingly at him.

Amelia didn't how much Mr Vishwanath had heard when she met the Princess. He had been there all the time, sitting on the other side of the room in one of his yoga positions. He was still sitting there in his yoga position when the Princess rushed out, and even after that he continued to sit for another couple of minutes. He certainly would have heard if he had been listening, but it was possible that he wasn't listening. Anyone else would have, but not Mr Vishwanath. He had once told Amelia that when he held one of his yoga poses he emptied his mind completely. Which was harder to do than it sounded, Amelia knew, because she had tried.

'Mr Vishwanath,' said Amelia, 'you don't understand.' Her voice dropped to a whisper, even though her father was too far away to hear, and even if he hadn't been, was too preoccupied with his machine to listen. 'I wrote a story. I read it to her.'

Amelia gazed at Mr Vishwanath, waiting to see how he would react. Just admitting it made her feel all the humiliation again. The Princess had called her story a fancy. A *fancy*! And then she had called it a stupid story. Amelia felt all the hurt once more. The Princess had made her feel so small, so foolish, like someone who didn't matter at all.

'Mr Vishwanath? Did you hear me?'

Mr Vishwanath nodded.

'She could at least have been polite, Mr Vishwanath. Even if she didn't like the story, she could have thanked me. She could have said she enjoyed it. But no. All she could say was it was a fancy.' Amelia forced out the word between gritted teeth, she could hardly bear to say it. 'All she cared about was the lamp! Did you hear her, Mr Vishwanath? All she wanted to know about was the lamp. And then she gets upset, and looks at me as if I don't even have the right to have a lamp. Why shouldn't I have a lamp? It's my lamp. She should get her own lamp!' Amelia folded her arms in outrage. 'I'll never write a story for anyone else again,' she muttered. 'Never. Do you hear me, Mr Vishwanath? Never!'

Mr Vishwanath didn't seem to have anything to say to that. Amelia turned angrily back to the garden, breathing heavily. Her father had managed to keep the machine upright with the latest sculpture and was wheeling it slowly towards the back. There were only a couple of the white sculptures left now. Amelia wasn't going to miss them when they were gone.

'Why is it important to you that the Princess cared about your story?'

Amelia looked at Mr Vishwanath in disbelief. Wasn't it obvious? He was still looking at the garden, and had spoken in that tone he sometimes had, that kind of murmur that made you wonder whether you really had heard anything at all or whether it was all in your own mind.

'Is it because you want to feel important?'

Mr Vishwanath's lips had hardly moved.

'It's not because I want to feel important.' Amelia's voice dropped again. 'Mr Vishwanath, you don't understand. I've never written a story for anyone before. I've never shown one to anyone. I've never even *told* anyone.' Amelia shook her head in frustration. 'Do you understand, Mr Vishwanath? Not one of my own stories.'

'How was the Princess to know this? Did you tell her?'

'It doesn't matter. She could have been polite, that's all. At least she could have said she enjoyed it.'

'What if she didn't enjoy it?'

'At least she could have thanked me for trying.'

'What if she didn't want you to try?'

'Mr Vishwanath, please. Sometimes when you do this . . . It just doesn't help.'

'When I do what, Amelia?'

'You know what I mean.'

'But I don't understand, Amelia. Would you prefer a person to lie just so you can feel important?'

Of course she didn't want someone to lie. But that wasn't the point. This wasn't about her feeling important. Somehow she couldn't get across to Mr

Vishwanath how hurt she felt, how much that story had meant to her.

'When we need other people to tell us we are important,' said Mr Vishwanath, 'we have lost sight of who we are. We do not know ourselves. We only know ourselves by what other people tell us.'

Why did Mr Vishwanath keep going on about that? It wasn't about being important!

Or was it? Amelia frowned. Suddenly she was starting to wonder. What *was* it about?

Really, why did it matter so much to her whether the Princess liked or disliked her story? What difference did that make to her, Amelia Dee? She was still Amelia Dee, and the story she had written was still exactly the same story that she had written, whether one particular princess happened to have disliked it. Another princess might have liked it, yet it would still be the same story, no better or worse, and she would still be the same Amelia Dee, and the other princess's opinion wouldn't matter either.

It was a good story, Amelia knew that, whatever anyone said. She didn't need to show it to anyone. She could have kept it hidden away, just like her mother kept her sculptures hidden in the garden, and it would be just as good. And she herself would be just as important – or just as unimportant – for having written it.

Amelia looked up at Mr Vishwanath. He was watching her.

'According to what you just said,' said Amelia, 'the Princess doesn't know herself.'

'What do you mean?' asked Mr Vishwanath.

'All she cares about is making sure everyone else treats her like she's an important person. I had to call her Your Serenity and she wasn't happy until I did. Why? Because that showed I wasn't as important as she is. If I was as important as her I could have used her real name. And that's what she wanted to prove.'

Mr Vishwanath didn't say anything to that.

'It's unfair!' said Amelia.

'To who?' asked Mr Vishwanath.

'To me! To anyone! To . . .' Amelia stopped. Suddenly, she wasn't sure.

Mr Vishwanath smiled. He turned back to look at the garden, where Amelia's father was very slowly, very carefully, beginning to winch another sculpture up on the machine.

'You're right about the Princess,' said Mr Vishwanath. 'She only cares about making sure she is treated importantly enough.'

'See?' said Amelia. 'That's unfair, isn't it?'

'It's much worse than unfair. It's a tragedy.'

Amelia wasn't sure about that. Calling it a tragedy might be taking it a *bit* far.

'It's the Princess's tragedy, Amelia.'

Amelia looked at Mr Vishwanath doubtfully. How could it be someone's tragedy that all they cared about was being treated importantly? If it was such a tragedy, why didn't they just stop caring about it?

Mr Vishwanath didn't explain.

Amelia thought about the Princess. She didn't like her, which made it hard to think of her as tragic. When you think of someone as tragic, you feel sympathy for them. But it was hard to think sympathetically of someone as unfriendly and ungrateful as the Princess.

Amelia tried to. She tried hard. It wasn't easy.

'I just don't know why you wanted me to meet her,' she said at last.

Mr Vishwanath shrugged. 'It's like a door. Sometimes you open a door, and maybe something will happen. Yes, Amelia?'

'And sometimes it doesn't.'

'Exactly,' replied Mr Vishwanath. 'One cannot tell.'

Amelia shook her head. 'You must have known what she'd be like, Mr Vishwanath. She's so spoiled! She wouldn't care about someone like me. I bet she lives in a *huge* palace with a whole *army* of servants and she gets *everything* she wants.'

Mr Vishwanath was silent.

Amelia stole a glance at him. Mr Vishwanath gazed imperturbably at the garden.

'The Princess does live in a palace, doesn't she?' asked Amelia eventually. 'I mean, in a house that's as big as a palace?'

Mr Vishwanath shook his head.

'But she's got servants, hasn't she? I mean, lots and lots?'

Mr Vishwanath shook his head again.

'That old man who drives for her . . . he's not the only one, is he?'

Mr Vishwanath didn't reply.

Amelia frowned. She remembered the tone of bitterness in the Princess's voice. She thought of the cream-coloured car that looked so impressive from a distance but so shoddy close up.

Somehow, Amelia realised, she had known what the answers to those questions would be, even as she asked them.

CHAPTER 11

In Eugenie's opinion, it must have been Amelia's fault. Amelia didn't tell Eugenie and Kevin about everything that happened with the Princess, because that would have meant telling them about the story she wrote, but she told them enough. And one thing was immediately apparent. To Eugenie, at least.

'You've ruined it! You realise that, don't you, Amelia? Not only for you, but for everyone!'

Amelia didn't know what she was talking about.

'If the Princess had liked you,' said Eugenie, 'she'd have asked you to bring a friend next time.'

'Like you, I suppose,' said Kevin.

Amelia sighed. 'Eugenie, there was never going to be a next time. Haven't you heard a thing I told you? The Princess doesn't normally meet children. She only did it because of Mr Vishwanath's suggestion.'

'But if she'd *liked* you, it would have been different, wouldn't it?'

Amelia glanced at Kevin and rolled her eyes in frustration.

'Did you do what I told you?' demanded Eugenie.

'Did you curtsy?'

Amelia shook her head.

'Hah! See?'

'And I didn't call her Your Highness, either.'

'Well, what do you *expect*?' cried Eugenie.

'She said I had to call her Your Serenity.'

'Oh.'

Kevin grinned.

Eugenie ignored him. 'And did you do that?'

'Yes,' said Amelia.

Eugenie narrowed her eyes. 'Every time?'

'Once or twice, anyway.'

'Hah!' cried Eugenie again. 'You have to say it every time you say something.'

'It wasn't that,' said Amelia.

'Then what was it?' demanded Eugenie. Suddenly she stopped, and gave Amelia a piercing glance. 'Did you take a gift?'

'She didn't want a gift.'

'But did you take one?'

Amelia frowned. She had no intention of saying anything about the story. It might have been different if the Princess had loved it, or even just liked it, or even just said something pleasant about it out of politeness. If that had happened, Amelia might have told Eugenie and Kevin about it, and even admitted that she had been writing stories for years. In a way, it would have

92

been a relief to tell them, and she had sometimes thought about doing it. But not now. All she'd get was the Martin Martinez treatment. Or worse.

Eugenie was still watching her keenly. Amelia could see that she knew there was something Amelia wasn't telling them.

'She was rude, that's all,' said Amelia abruptly, and she marched off.

Eugenie and Kevin ran to catch up with her.

They went into the Froot Jus bar. Eugenie kept glancing at Amelia as they waited to be served.

'What?' whispered Amelia.

'She was the rude one, was she?' said Eugenie. 'That was the problem, was it? Nothing *you* might have done?'

Obviously, for Eugenie Edelstein, a princess could do no wrong, and if there was ever a problem it had to be someone else's fault.

'Yes, she was,' said Amelia. 'Rude. She said she didn't like meeting children because they behave disgracefully. She said it to my face without even waiting to see how I behaved!'

'She'd already seen, I think.'

'Once! That was only once, Eugenie. She was the one who behaved disgracefully this time.'

Eugenie glanced at Amelia pitifully, as if there were something very, very sad about a girl who could delude herself as to who was to blame in such a situation.

The man behind the counter was ready to serve them. Kevin got a mango and banana smoothie. Amelia got a blackcurrant, gooseberry and papaya crush. And Eugenie, after carefully examining every option on the board, got a cucumber juice.

They sat down.

'It's peculiar,' said Amelia, staring thoughtfully at Eugenie's drink.

'No, it's not! I love cucumber juice,' retorted Eugenie, and she grimaced as she took a sip.

'No, what Mr Vishwanath said to me afterwards. He said the Princess was always worried about whether people were treating her importantly enough, and that was her tragedy.'

Eugenie shook her head dismissively. 'That's just Mr Vishwanath.'

'What's that supposed to mean?' demanded Amelia.

'Nothing.'

'What?' demanded Amelia again.

'It's just . . . he's odd, Amelia. Admit it.'

'He's not odd.'

'Of course he is. How many students does he have, not counting the Princess? Yet he sends people away. If that's not odd, I don't know what is.'

'You have to admit,' said Kevin, 'it is odd.'

'Mr Vishwanath doesn't care about money,' replied Amelia.

'See?' Eugenie threw up her hands. 'What more proof do you need?'

Amelia sucked on her straw. She knew that people said Mr Vishwanath was odd – when they weren't saying even worse things. She wished she could stop them. But she knew Mr Vishwanath himself wouldn't care. She could just imagine what he would say if she told him. It wouldn't worry him, not even for a second.

'It would be like a fly sitting on his hand,' said Amelia.

'What would?' asked Eugenie.

'If you told him you think he's odd. He wouldn't even notice it was there. And if he did notice, he would gently brush it away. He wouldn't try to kill it, because it's so unimportant it wouldn't even be worth it. He'd just brush it away and not give it another moment's thought.'

'Amelia!' exclaimed Eugenie. 'That's awful! We should always worry about what other people think of us! My mother says that's the most important thing.'

Kevin frowned. That explained quite a lot.

'Does Mr Vishwanath really say that?' asked Eugenie.

'Yes,' said Amelia. He would, if anyone asked him. In fact, Amelia was feeling quite pleased with herself for thinking of it. It was exactly the way Mr Vishwanath would put it.

'You mustn't listen to him, Amelia. You really mustn't.'

Amelia shrugged.

'I'm serious!'

'I know you are,' said Amelia, and she exchanged a look with Kevin.

They sipped their juices. Eugenie kept glancing longingly at Amelia's and Kevin's drinks, but whenever they noticed, she took a big, wincing sip of her cucumber juice, as if nothing could be more delicious.

A couple came in and bought juices and sat down at a table. They kept holding each other's hand and kissing. They hardly had time to drink their drinks because of all the kissing they were doing. Eugenie could barely take her eyes off them. Kevin and Amelia glanced at each other and grinned.

'Come on, Eugenie,' said Amelia eventually. 'Let's go.'

'What?'

'Come on,' said Kevin. 'Haven't you seen anyone kiss before?'

Eugenie looked at him angrily. 'I wasn't watching them kiss.'

'Well, I don't know what else you were watching,' said Amelia, 'because that's all they've been doing!'

The couple heard and looked at them sharply.

Amelia smiled, and walked out of the shop.

'I wasn't watching them kiss!' said Eugenie again when they were outside.

'Whatever,' said Amelia.

'I wasn't!'

'Why do you care so much even if you were?' asked Kevin.

Eugenie glared at him, then refused to answer.

They headed home.

'Well, I hope you're happy,' said Eugenie after a while. 'You've ruined it, Amelia, absolutely ruined it for all of us.'

Kevin rolled his eyes. 'You're not back on the Princess again, are you?'

'If only you'd done what I told you.'

'Eugenie,' muttered Kevin, 'let it go.'

'Was it too hard for you to bring her a gift? Was that really too hard?'

Amelia took a deep breath, trying to hold herself back. Even though Eugenie Edelstein was one of her two best friends, there were times when Eugenie was absolutely insufferable and Amelia wondered how she had ever ended up being friends with her at all. Like now. Moments like now made her wonder how you ever could become friends with anyone and not end up wanting to kill them.

Amelia glanced at her. Eugenie glanced back, and put her nose in the air.

'Well, I'm sorry!' said Amelia. 'You won't get the chance to meet her, alright? So just live with it.' And Amelia put her nose in the air as well, to show Eugenie that two could play at that game.

They turned the corner into Marburg Street.

'Ummm . . . you might,' said Kevin.

'What?' demanded Eugenie.

'Get the chance to meet her.'

Amelia and Eugenie dropped their noses and looked.

The cream-coloured car was parked outside the green house of Solomon Weiszacker. It was in exactly the place where it always parked when the Princess came for her yoga sessions, and the driver was in the front seat, just as he always was. Yet there was something unusual about the scene. The Princess, who normally got out and went straight into Mr Vishwanath's studio, was in the car as well. Sitting in the back seat. As if she was waiting for somebody.

CHAPTER 12

The driver got out of the car. He put on his hat and carefully adjusted it on his head and then he stood up straight – or as straight as he could, because he was quite bent with age – in front of Amelia and her two friends.

'Her Serenity the Princess Parvin Kha-Douri,' he announced solemnly, 'has the honour to beg a favour of the Mademoiselle Amelia Dee.' He spoke in an accent similar to that of the Princess, although stronger. When he said Amelia's name, he pronounced it 'Ehmeeelieh', just as she had.

Amelia glanced at Eugenie, who was obviously as jealous as anything of the fact that Amelia had just been called a mademoiselle by a princess. Or at least by a princess's driver.

'Will you grant the Princess this favour?' said the driver.

'You'd better ask what it is first,' whispered Kevin.

'Her Serenity the Princess Parvin Kha-Douri requests of the Mademoiselle Amelia Dee the favour of seeing the lamp.'

'The lamp?' said Amelia.

The man nodded. 'The peacock lamp.'

'The lamp that I . . .' Amelia paused, conscious that Eugenie and Kevin were hanging on every word. 'The lamp that that I mentioned to her?'

The man frowned. 'Please wait a minute.' He turned around and opened the back door of the car and there was a hurried conversation between himself and the Princess.

'Amelia,' whispered Eugenie suspiciously. 'What lamp is this? You didn't tell us you mentioned any lamp.'

The man closed the door and turned around again. He drew himself up to his full, bent height. He was such a small man to begin with, and so hunched with age, that he stood hardly taller than Amelia herself.

'Her Serenity the Princess Parvin Kha-Douri requests of the Mademoiselle Amelia Dee the favour of seeing the lamp that she mentioned, if, indeed, it is hanging in her house.'

'It is hanging in her house,' said Amelia.

'Then Her Serenity requests the favour to see it.'

'Now?' said Amelia.

'If this would be convenient,' said the man.

Amelia really didn't know why she should let the Princess see the lamp, after the Princess had been so horrible to her. She looked at the car and saw the

100

Princess watching her from the back seat. Their eyes met. At first, all Amelia saw in the Princess's gaze was insistence, an expectation of obedience, the look of someone who thought she had a right to be granted what she was asking. Exactly what you would expect from someone like the Princess. Then Amelia sensed that maybe there was something else there as well, something less certain in the Princess's gaze, almost tentative, imploring. Maybe. Maybe it was only because it was so unexpected to see that in the Princess's eyes that Amelia wasn't sure whether it was there at all.

Amelia turned back to the man. 'Alright,' she said.

The man nodded. He turned around and opened the car door and said something. Then he stood back.

'Her Serenity the Princess Parvin Kha-Douri,' he announced solemnly.

Out of the car came the Princess. She was wearing her fur coat, as usual. Amelia wondered what was underneath it this time. Not the green yoga leotard. Or maybe it was the green leotard. Maybe that was all the Princess ever wore, a fur coat and leotard.

For an instant, Eugenie stared. Then she dropped into the lowest, most flamboyant curtsy imaginable, arms spread, head bowed, face down, her nose just about touching the pavement.

'This is my friend, Eugenie Edelstein,' said Amelia.

Eugenie dropped even lower, if that was possible.

'And this is Kevin Chan,' said Amelia.

'Hello,' said Kevin.

The Princess glanced at them for the briefest time imaginable. Then she looked at Amelia again. And Amelia could see that already she had put Kevin and Eugenie out of her mind – if they had even got into her mind – and as far as the Princess was concerned they were just two more people who had been introduced to her at some point during her life, and it could just as easily have happened a week ago, or a year ago, or ten years ago, as a minute ago, for all the difference it made to her.

'I would be very grateful, Mademoiselle,' she said stiffly to Amelia, 'if I might see the lamp.'

It crossed Amelia's mind that now was the time to tell the Princess she couldn't see it. Now, after she had got out of the car. That would be humiliating. Perhaps not as humiliating as the way the Princess had treated her, but it would be something, at least.

She considered it for a moment. But she didn't do it.

'Follow me,' said Amelia.

She led the Princess into the house through the door under Solomon Weiszacker's plaque. Kevin followed, and so did Eugenie, after she finally got up from her curtsy. The Princess's driver stayed outside with the car.

'Through here,' said Amelia, leading the Princess

down the hall. She got to the bottom of the stairs. 'It's up there.'

Amelia flicked the switch at the bottom of the stairs. The light came on high above them, and the stairwell filled with the lamp's soft, warm, stippled glow.

The Princess looked up. Amelia folded her arms and waited.

'Amelia!' said Mrs Ellis, bustling out of the kitchen. 'I don't think we need the light on in the middle of the day! How many times do I have to—'

Mrs Ellis stopped.

'This is Her Serenity the Princess Parvin Kha-Douri,' said Eugenie quickly, probably hoping the Princess would say she was grateful and call her a mademoiselle, as she had called Amelia.

'And this is Mrs Ellis,' said Amelia to the Princess.

Mrs Ellis stared in confusion. Then she did a little curtsy, which was much the strangest thing Amelia had seen on what was turning out to be a pretty strange day.

'Of course, if you want to put it on . . .' Mrs Ellis mumbled. 'I mean . . . Your Serenity . . . naturally . . .'

'Amelia!' said her father, coming in from the back door. 'Where have you been? I called you before to—' He stopped. 'Oh. Who's this?'

The Princess looked at him.

'Her Serenity the Princess Parvin Kha-Douri,' said Amelia. 'This is my father.'

The Princess nodded.

'She's come to see the lamp.'

'The lamp?' said Amelia's father.

Amelia pointed towards the ceiling at the top of the stairs.

'If I may see it,' said the Princess.

'Oh. Of course,' said Amelia's father. 'You're very welcome to see it. It's just a lamp, though. A beautiful lamp, but just a lamp.'

The Princess's eyes narrowed.

'There's nothing particularly special . . . I mean technically . . . and it's not as if there's any kind of a story . . .'

Amelia's father's voice trailed away. The Princess had turned from him, and was gazing upwards once more.

He leaned closer to Amelia. 'What's going on?'

'Amelia mentioned the lamp to the Princess, Mr Dee,' whispered Kevin.

'When?'

'When she met her.'

Amelia's father frowned. 'You've met this Princess, Amelia? When?'

A huge crash came from behind the door of the sculpture room on the second floor, followed by an ear-piercing wail of frustration.

The Princess looked at Amelia, as if awoken from

her thoughts. 'I would like to see the lamp more closely, if I may.'

'You mean you want to go up?' asked Amelia.

'If you would allow me.'

Amelia glanced at her father. He shrugged.

'Why not?' said Amelia.

'Does that mean I may?' asked the Princess.

'Yes,' said Amelia.

The Princess nodded. 'Thank you,' she said. She moved to the stairs, then stopped, noticing the first of the paintings that lined the wall of the staircase.

'It's my mother's,' said Amelia. 'They all are.'

One of the Princess's eyebrows rose a fraction. Then she put her foot on the first step.

'Um . . .' Amelia's father coughed. 'You might want to watch out for the wires. On the stairs. Nothing to worry about . . . it's just . . . work in progress . . .'

The Princess looked down. Her eyebrow rose higher. Carefully, she started up the stairs.

The Princess ascended slowly. Behind her came Amelia, Kevin, Eugenie, Amelia's father and Mrs Ellis, all in a kind of procession.

As they got to the second floor, the door of the sculpture room opened, and out came Amelia's mother in her sculpting smock, covered in white stone dust.

'How can I work?' she yelled. 'All these footsteps! These foot—' She stopped.

'This is Her Serenity the Princess Parvin Kha-Douri,' said Eugenie.

'Oh,' said Amelia's mother.

The Princess nodded at her.

'She's come to see the lamp,' said Amelia's father, and he glanced upwards to show her which lamp he meant.

'Oh,' said Amelia's mother again. 'I've been . . . Excuse me,' she said, suddenly becoming aware of how she must look in her dust-covered smock with her dust-covered face and dust-covered hair. 'I've been sculpting.'

'How nice,' said the Princess evenly.

'Having a bit of trouble, I'm afraid.'

'How unfortunate,' said the Princess, and started up the next flight of stairs.

Everyone followed. Amelia's mother joined the end of the procession and went up the stairs as well.

They stopped at the top, outside the door to Amelia's room. The lamp hung from its chains a metre or so above the banister. Only from this close, as Amelia knew, could you appreciate how big the lamp really was, and how intricate the metalwork.

The Princess gazed at the lamp. Seconds passed, then minutes. The Princess continued to stare, hardly even blinked.

Amelia frowned. What was going on?

She thought about how she had swung on the lamp. That was a long time ago. No one knew about it.

The Princess continued to stare. Not a word. Amelia glanced at Eugenie and Kevin. The whole situation was starting to feel quite odd.

Amelia's father cleared his throat. 'We don't know where it came from,' he said. 'Or how long it's been here. It's not an original feature, though. If you look right up you can tell from the way it's been fitted to the ceiling. See how the chains have been attached?'

The Princess didn't look right up. There was nothing to show she had heard a single word Amelia's father had said.

He laughed nervously. 'Afraid we can't tell you anything about it. Nothing at all. Wish we knew someone who could. Right, Amelia? Amelia?'

'Yes,' said Amelia, who just wished her father would stop talking. He had a habit of talking when he didn't know what was going on, as if filling the air with sound would make things clearer. Usually it did the opposite.

'Yes,' said Amelia's father. 'Nothing at all. Must be quite a story, I'm sure. Or maybe not.' He gave another short laugh. 'But there we are! A mystery.'

Amelia watched the Princess. She was utterly, utterly uninterested in anything going on around her. The lamp took her entire attention.

'Well,' said Amelia's father. He clapped his hands

briskly. 'I think we've probably spent enough time—'

'There were six in the palace,' murmured the Princess. 'Each one different.'

'Pardon?' said Amelia's father. 'I didn't quite catch that.'

But the Princess wasn't talking to him. She was talking to herself, or to someone else, perhaps, who existed only in her mind.

'One in each of the children's rooms,' she murmured, 'even the youngest.'

The Princess was silent again.

'Who was the youngest?' asked Amelia quietly.

The Princess smiled to herself, still gazing at the lamp. 'Me.'

There were footsteps on the stairs. It was the Princess's driver. He was coming up slowly, holding his hat in his hands, with the hesitant steps of a person who isn't quite sure if he should be doing what he's doing.

As he came up the last stairs, the Princess looked down at him. The driver stopped.

'Do you see, Asha?' said the Princess.

The man nodded, and kept coming. He reached the landing where everyone was standing.

'Do you see?' said the Princess again, turning back to the lamp.

'Yes, my Princess. I see.'

'It is the peacock lamp. See? See them? And look, the monkeys. There they are, on the side. There. Do you remember how Ali El stood on his ladder and held me up so I could see them?'

'Yes, my Princess. I remember.'

'And I couldn't see them. But Ali El showed me, and then I could. To find a monkey, you must look for the curve in the tail. Then follow the tail and you will find the rest of him. Do you remember, Asha?'

'Yes, my Princess.'

'And the one with the face of a person. That was supposed to be the face of Ramzi Ghav. Everyone laughed when they found out. Do you remember, Asha?'

'Yes, my Princess.'

The driver smiled apologetically at Amelia's mother and father, as if to beg them to excuse his mistress.

'Here it is. My lamp. Here, in this plain little house. Why, Asha?'

'It's not such a little house,' said Amelia's father.

'And it's hardly plain,' added her mother.

Asha looked at them apologetically again, spreading his hands helplessly.

'Why is it here, Asha? Why?'

Asha turned back to the Princess. 'I do not know, my Princess. Come away. You have seen it. Come away now, my Princess. What good does it do to torment yourself?'

'But it is here!'

'Yes,' said the driver.

'It is here, Asha!'

'Yes, but it does not change anything, my Princess. Nothing will change anything.'

Amelia's father leaned close to Amelia. 'You don't think she wants us to give her the lamp, do you?'

Amelia watched the Princess. She almost thought she saw tears in the old lady's eyes.

'Come,' said Asha.

But the Princess made no movement. The driver, who might have put a hand on her arm to lead her away, stood by, obviously unwilling to touch her.

He looked around and smiled his apologetic smile again, as someone who had long been accustomed to seeking forgiveness for the whims of his mistress.

The Princess continued to gaze at the lamp, lost in her thoughts.

'She said there were six in the palace,' said Amelia. 'Did she mean six lamps?'

Asha nodded.

'Which palace?' asked Amelia.

'The palace where she was born,' replied the driver. He glanced at the Princess again, but she was oblivious to all.

'What palace was that?'

'The Grand Palace of Ervahan.' Asha sighed. 'Such a palace, Mademoiselle Amelia! I was her servant there. Young. Young almost like the Princess.'

'And you're still her servant,' said Amelia. 'The last one?'

Asha bowed his head. 'She is my Princess.'

'Loyalty,' murmured Amelia's father, nodding approvingly. 'Very good.'

'Where is the Grand Palace of Ervahan?' asked Amelia.

Asha shook his head. He glanced anxiously at the Princess, then held a finger to his lips. 'It no longer exists,' he whispered.

'Nothing?'

'Nothing,' said Asha, and he held his finger to his lips again.

Amelia nodded.

Her father leaned close to her. 'Maybe we should give her the lamp. What do you think?'

Asha looked at Amelia. His eyes were full of despair. 'She is exile. Since a little girl. Since the revolution, she has never been back to our country. She can now, for many years she can, but it is too much. Too bitter.' He smiled sadly. 'Too bitter.'

The Princess frowned, staring at the lamp. Then her head quivered briefly, as if some memory had just run through her mind, a memory she couldn't quite believe. And then another.

'Come, my Princess,' said Asha. He took a step closer to the Princess, and spoke to her, this time in a language Amelia didn't understand. Still he didn't dare to touch her, to wake her from reverie.

He spoke to her again. Suddenly the Princess looked around. For a moment she stared at the people watching her, as if she had forgotten where she was. Her eyes were moist.

She turned away, so that no one could see her face,

and put out her hand and muttered something very quickly. Asha handed her a handkerchief. She dried her eyes, still facing the wall, then held out the hand-kerchief. Asha took it. She turned back.

She had recovered her poise now. 'I am very grateful,' she said. Her voice was controlled, her expression almost haughty. 'Mademoiselle Amelia, you have been most gracious in allowing me to see your lamp. Madame Dee, Monsieur Dee, I thank you also.'

Amelia's father nodded, and then he didn't know what to do, so he nodded again, and the nod turned into a kind of bow.

'You're very welcome,' said Amelia's mother.

'Come, Asha!' said the Princess. 'We go!'

She headed down the stairs. Everyone followed. Down the hall she went, out the door. Asha opened the back door of the car for her.

'Thank you. Goodbye,' said the Princess.

Eugenie dropped in one of her exaggerated curtsies as the Princess got into the car.

Asha closed the door behind her. He smiled his apologetic smile. 'Thank you,' he said. 'This means much to my Princess, to see the lamp.' He went around the car and opened his own door. 'Thank you,' he said again before he got in.

The car started, and a moment later it moved off.

On the pavement, Eugenie was still curtsying.

113

Kevin Chan rolled his eyes. 'Eugenie, what are you doing? She never said one word to you!'

It was true, everything the Princess's driver had said. There really had been a palace in an ancient city called Ervahan, and there had been a revolution, and the palace had been destroyed, and the family that had ruled the country had been driven into exile. Amelia had checked.

She found it in a book. The only clue she had was the name of the city, Ervahan, and she didn't even know where Ervahan was. But the school librarian helped her track it down. It was in a country called Irafia. The book they found was called *A History of Irafia*, and went back hundreds and hundreds of years. It wasn't an easy book to read, written in a very dry, uninteresting fashion, but it was bloodcurdling enough, with deception and violence and murderous wars on a monumental scale. Princes always seemed to be plotting against the ruler of the country to get hold of the throne, only to be plotted against themselves. The stories of treachery and bloodshed in the book would have been as scary as anything Amelia had ever read if only the whole thing had been written more excitingly. Way back, about three hundred years ago, a pair of princes had actually managed to stab each other to death in a fight for the throne. That just meant a whole lot of their younger brothers started fighting and set off a fresh series of wars. Finally, in the last century, a very intelligent man came to power and united the country, and there had been peace. But his son wasn't as wise, according to the book, and besides, by the time he came to the throne, the people were beginning to question whether they should be ruled without having any right to choose their ruler, and one thing led to another, dissatisfaction led to more dissatisfaction, and eventually, fifty-nine years earlier, there had been a revolution.

That was the part that really surprised Amelia. There was nothing unusual about all the tales of war and betrayal. History was full of stories like that. And revolutions as well. But only fifty-nine years ago? The revolutions Amelia knew about, like the French Revolution, and the American Revolution, had happened hundreds of years ago. That was when history happened, long ago. Yet fifty-nine years . . . Fifty-nine years wasn't that long. It was long, but not *that* long. There were plenty of people still alive who could remember things that happened fifty-nine years ago. Amelia's Dee grandparents, on her father's side, for example, and her Arbuckle grandparents on her mother's side. Although her grandfather Arbuckle on her mother's side had become very forgetful in the past couple of years and sometimes forgot Amelia's name. When that happened, everyone laughed quickly and pretended he hadn't really forgotten, and was just playing a game, but Amelia knew he really had forgotten, and every time she saw him he seemed to forget more. But Amelia knew that he was over eighty years old, and looked even older, so if his memory hadn't got so bad he would easily have been able to remember what had happened fifty-nine years earlier.

And yet the history book spoke about the Irafian revolution just like any other revolution that had happened hundreds of years in the past. It gave the names of the family that had been removed from power, the Shan and Shanna – which were the titles the Irafians used for their king and queen – and their six children. The youngest was Princess Parvin. Parvin! There she was, in a book about history, just like some dead person. Yet she wasn't some dead person from history. She was a live person who turned up, fifty-nine years later, in a fur coat over a green leotard to do yoga with Mr Vishwanath on the ground floor of Amelia's house. She scowled and was haughty and then looked at a lamp and cried. And yet, at the same time, she was a person from history as well.

It made Amelia think of all the people she had heard about in history: Julius Caesar and Napoleon and

Galileo and Captain Cook and Florence Nightingale and Christopher Columbus and Madame Curie and Joan of Arc. Suddenly she realised they weren't really anything more than names to her. But they hadn't been just names, not when they were alive. They had been real people, with real personalities. Some must have been nice, some nasty, some friendly, some prickly. They must have had real feelings. They must have laughed sometimes, and cried, and had foods they liked to eat and foods they couldn't bear, and maybe they sang to themselves in the bath. When things happened to them – all the things that happened in history – they must have felt real pain, or real pleasure, just as Amelia herself felt when things happened to her.

What happened in the Irafian revolution, according to the book, was that the Shan didn't want to allow the people to have any say in choosing who would be in the government. He wanted to choose the government himself. In fact, instead of allowing the people to have some choice, which might have kept them happy, he tried to take away even the small amount of choice they already had, and he became more and more brutal as the people resisted. It was complicated, and Amelia wasn't sure she understood it all. There was also some kind of disagreement with officers in the army about the way the Shan was talking to the leaders of some other countries which they regarded as enemies.

Eventually it all exploded in a revolution. A number of people died, and the Shan and the Shanna themselves might have been killed had they not been secretly spirited out of the country on a boat, together with their six children, by a loyal captain. They had no time to pack or prepare, and could take with them only what they could carry. When news spread that they had fled, the violence got even worse. Looting and riots broke out. The Grand Palace in Ervahan, parts of which were more than a thousand years old, was burned to the ground.

Eventually the army seized control and restored order, leading to a kind of military government. The Shan himself continued to create trouble from exile, living on money he had illegally put away in foreign banks and encouraging people in Irafia to rebel so he could reclaim his throne. But he never succeeded in returning, and died eighteen years later. His wife, the Shanna, lived on another fourteen years. As for the six children, the book didn't say what happened to them.

Amelia told all of this to Kevin and Eugenie when they were in the café at the cinema, waiting to see a film. There were about a hundred other kids in there, noisily waiting as well.

Kevin frowned, toying with the straw in the milkshake he had just finished. 'That's amazing,' he murmured.

Eugenie nodded. 'Poor Princess.'

Yes, thought Amelia. Poor Princess. She was just a child when she was driven from the palace, chased out by an angry mob. Probably no older than Amelia herself.

'And the lamp in your house was from the palace,' said Kevin.

'I didn't know that before,' said Amelia.

'Then why did you tell her about it?'

'I just mentioned it when I met her.'

'Why?'

'I don't know. It doesn't matter.'

'Yes, it does,' said Eugenie.

Amelia glanced at her. Eugenie had that look in her eyes again. She knew Amelia was hiding something.

'Tell us exactly what you said.'

'It was nothing.' Amelia turned back to Kevin. 'They must have looted it before the palace burned down. The book said there was looting.'

'But how does it get here? All the way from Irafia to your house?'

Amelia shrugged. 'No one knows who installed it.'

'It's amazing.'

'No, it's not,' said Eugenie impatiently. 'Someone loots it. Then they sell it. Then they sell it to some-one else.'

'All the way from Irafia?'

'What's so surprising?' Eugenie's uncle had an antiques shop which was full of things from other countries. 'People bring my uncle all kinds of stuff.'

'How does he knew it isn't stolen?'

'When someone brings him something he always asks for proof they bought it or inherited it. I've asked him. He won't take it if they can't show him. But he admits there's no way of knowing whether whoever they bought it or inherited it from didn't steal it themselves. According to Uncle Randolph, somewhere along the line, maybe even hundreds of years ago, a lot of stuff in antiques shops has been stolen, but there's nothing anyone can do about it.'

'I suppose that explains how the lamp got to my house,' said Amelia.

'But it still doesn't explain how you came to mention it to the Princess,' said Eugenie, which was what she was really interested in.

Amelia sighed. 'It's not important, Eugenie.'

Eugenie looked at her knowingly, then stuck her nose in the air.

Behind them, people were coming out of the cinema into the lobby. The first session was finished. Kids around them in the café were already getting up to go in for the next session.

Eugenie frowned. 'Imagine losing everything like that. One minute you're living in the lap of luxury, the next minute you're running away with nothing but what you can carry.'

'True,' said Kevin, 'but look at it from the other perspective. One minute you're a poor person with some Shan and Shanna controlling you're life, the next minute you're free.'

Eugenie shook her head.

'Eugenie, think about it. If the people revolted, they couldn't have been happy. I bet the Shan and Shanna made life pretty hard for everyone.'

'That wasn't the Princess's fault. She was just a child.'

'I'm not saying it was her fault. But the only reason she could live in luxury was because of that.'

'So you're saying they had the right to take everything she had? To take her palace? Even her lamp?'

'I'm saying the people had a right to something.'

'The lamp was hers, Kevin.'

'Yeah, but look at it another way, and the lamp was really theirs.'

'The lamp's mine now,' said Amelia. 'That's the funny thing.'

There was silence for a moment.

'You're just jealous,' said Eugenie to Kevin.

'Of what?'

'Of everything the Princess had. You don't like the

122

idea she had it all because you could never have anything like it yourself.'

'That's not true. I'm just saying, you can understand why the people would have been angry.'

Eugenie smiled smugly, as if she knew what was *really* going on in Kevin's mind.

'Why do you want to defend her?' demanded Kevin in exasperation. 'Why do you take her side? Eugenie, she was horrible. She didn't say a word to you the other day.'

'She did.'

'She didn't.'

'She did!'

'She didn't. For all she cared, you weren't so much as a speck of dust.'

'That's not true!'

'Amelia? Did the Princess say a word to Eugenie?'

Amelia shook her head. The Princess hadn't said a word to Eugenie, as they all knew.

'Well, what do you expect?' demanded Eugenie. 'She's had such a terrible life. Everything was taken away from her. How old was she? No older than we are. Just imagine it, suddenly you have to leave, and you can't take anything with you.'

'She obviously managed to keep something,' said Kevin.

'What's that supposed to mean?'

'Well, look at her. She's got that big car. She must have had the money to buy that. And there's the old guy who drives her around. He was her servant all the way back then. I bet he's stayed with her all his life.'

'Yeah, and I bet it's nothing compared with the life they left behind. One old car. One old servant. Imagine how many servants she must have had in the Grand Palace!'

Kevin shook his head. 'Maybe they only managed to take what they could carry, but they had money somewhere, didn't they? Isn't that what you said, Amelia? In a bank or something? And where did that money come from? It was illegally put there by the Shan. So whose was it really?'

'See!' cried Eugenie. 'You *are* jealous. Look at him, Amelia. He's as jealous as anything.'

'I'm not jealous! I just don't think the Princess has had such a terrible life. She could have gone back if she wanted.'

'There was a revolution!'

'After the revolution. She could go back now, the old guy said so. But she won't, will she? Why? Because she won't be a princess any more, and that's all she cares about. Having people call her Your Serenity. I bet no one will call her Your Serenity in Irafia. Right, Amelia?'

Amelia nodded. It was true. All the Princess cared about was being treated according to her rank, and treating other people according to theirs. And Kevin hadn't seen how horrible she could really be in the way she treated people, not as Amelia had seen it that day in Mr Vishwanath's studio.

'She could still say hello to us, couldn't she?' said Kevin. 'She could still be civil. I bet she'd have a lot more friends if she did.'

'A princess doesn't want friends,' retorted Eugenie. 'If you knew anything about princesses, you'd realise that. But you don't know the first thing about them. How can you possibly know what it is to be a princess and then to have all of it, everything, taken away?'

True as well, thought Amelia. None of them could really know what that would be like.

Kevin and Eugenie glared at each other.

Amelia frowned. In a way, they each had a point.

She looked around. The café was empty. The film must have started. Everyone had gone in.

The lamp hung motionless above the stairs. Amelia switched it on, and it glowed. She switched it off. She switched it on and off again a couple of times, quickly.

She traced the metalwork with her eyes, as she had traced it hundreds of times before. Each swirl and curve seemed to flow into another, but Amelia knew how to find the shapes within them. Focus on the mass of detail, and everything dissolved into endless intricacy, but focus on the individual shapes, and the detail around them slipped away. You could see nothing in the fine metalwork of the lamp, or all kinds of things, depending on how you looked at it.

Her lamp. That was how she had always thought of it. It was because of this lamp that she had started writing stories. And whenever she felt that maybe that was a silly thing to do, and people would laugh if they knew, she only had to gaze at the lamp, lose herself amongst the familiar shapes hidden in the bronze, and she knew there was nothing silly about it at all.

But it wasn't just her lamp. It was something else now. It was someone else's as well. Or had been.

Amelia saw it in a way she had never seen it before. Not just the metalwork itself, but everything the lamp represented. Where it had come from. What it had been.

What if the Princess wanted it back? What if she could prove that it had been hers, and that she had a right to it?

Amelia switched it on again, and the lamp glowed.

There had been six in the palace, the Princess had said. Amelia tried to imagine the lamp hanging in the palace. A lamp of that size must have hung high, she thought, right in the centre of a room. She tried to imagine what the room looked like. What were its walls made of? Marble? Wood? What kind of windows? Square ones? Arched ones? She didn't know. The book about Irafia didn't have any pictures of the Grand Palace of Ervahan. It had a picture of the Shan, who had been overthrown, and of a man who had replaced him as president of the new republic. The Shan had a long face with a deep crease in each cheek. The man who replaced him was plumper, almost a jolly-looking man. But his looks deceived. According to the book, he was brutal, as brutal as the Shan himself, and had ordered hundreds of the Shan's supporters to be executed. He himself had ruled for only three years before being overthrown.

Amelia tried to imagine what the palace must have

been like. It must have been very grand, to judge by the lamp. Amelia smiled. That's what people would say about her house, if the only thing left from it was the lamp that was hanging in front of her. 'It must have been a *very* grand house,' they would say, 'if it had lamps like that!' But that was wrong because the lamp didn't really belong in her house. It hadn't been made for it. Yet the lamp had belonged in the palace at Ervahan. And if a lamp like that belonged there – and not just one lamp, but six of them – what other things there must have been!

Amelia gazed at the lamp. What other things there must have been, she thought.

Eugenie was right, it would have been terrible to lose all of that. Imagine growing up in a such a place, and suddenly, one night, having to run away and get on a boat to save your life from a mob, taking nothing but what you could carry. Even if your family still had some wealth afterwards, it would never be the same. You would never have that kind of luxury again. Not only a palace, but a whole country you could call your own.

But that didn't necessarily make it fair for the Princess to have had all those things in the first place. Maybe it was Kevin who was right. The things the Princess and her family had – the luxury, the palaces, the lamps, everything – maybe they should never have had them in the first place. When the people took those things away, they were just taking back what was actually theirs.

Amelia sighed. She put her elbows on the banister and looked up at the lamp, picking out the two fan-tailed peacocks on the bottom. Eugenie and Kevin were both right. That was the problem. It depended on how you looked at it. From the perspective of the Princess, it was terribly sad. And yet if you looked at it from the perspective of the people of Irafia, it wasn't sad at all. Quite the opposite.

It was confusing. No matter how much she thought about it – and she had thought about it a lot – Amelia didn't quite feel that she completely understood it, that she could make one perspective fit with the other. She didn't think she had come across a problem before in which the opposite sides of the argument both seemed to be right. At least she couldn't remember one. And she was pretty sure she would have, considering how much trouble this one was giving her!

It didn't seem to surprise Mr Vishwanath. He listened as she explained the conundrum, sitting in his chair under the back verandah, gazing at the garden. There were no sculptures in the garden now. Amelia's father had removed the white ones, and Amelia's mother hadn't yet revealed anything new. She was working furiously, though, enclosed behind the door of her sculpture room, from which came a steady stream of bangs and crashes.

But the shouts of frustration had more or less stopped. Amelia's father said that meant she had finally worked out what her new phase was going to be about, and at last she was actually creating something.

Mr Vishwanath nodded when Amelia finished telling him how confusing it was.

Amelia waited for him to respond. But he didn't.

'You must have something to say, Mr Vishwanath,' said Amelia at last.

'No.'

'But it's so confusing!'

'It is what it is,' said Mr Vishwanath.

'What does that mean?'

'Everything in life is like this,' murmured Mr Vishwanath.

'No it isn't!' replied Amelia. 'Nothing in life is like this. I've never come across anything like it before.'

'Then you haven't thought enough about the things you have come across.'

'Well, if everything in life's like this, how do you ever know what's right?' demanded Amelia.

Mr Vishwanath glanced at her. He smiled that gentle, questioning smile of his. Amelia knew what was coming next. Something she wouldn't understand, probably.

'When you *know* you are right, that is the time you can be sure you are wrong,' said Mr Vishwanath quietly.

'Mr Vishwanath,' demanded Amelia, 'how can that be right? If you *know* you're right . . .'

Something in Mr Vishwanath's gaze made Amelia stop. He looked at her for a moment longer, then turned back to the garden.

Amelia frowned. It didn't seem to make sense, and yet there was something in Mr Vishwanath's remark that seemed to say: 'Think about me a little longer, I'm not nonsense'. If a remark could talk, of course.

There was silence.

'She came to visit us,' said Amelia.

'Who came to visit you?' asked Mr Vishwanath.

'The Princess.'

Mr Vishwanath turned. Amelia had never seen Mr Vishwanath look surprised. He didn't look surprised now, but he nearly did, and for Mr Vishwanath, that probably meant he had just had the shock of his life.

Amelia smiled. That was something, shocking Mr Vishwanath.

'A couple of days ago,' said Amelia. 'Didn't you see her?'

Mr Vishwanath shook his head.

'She wanted to see the lamp. The lamp I mentioned in the story I wrote for her. Turns out . . .' Amelia paused, wanting to see if she could surprise

131

Mr Vishwanath even more. 'It used to hang in her palace!'

Amelia watched him closely, trying to see what effect she had had.

Mr Vishwanath turned back to the garden. 'In the palace where she was born?' he asked.

'Yes.'

'What did she say?'

'Not much. She just looked at it. The palace doesn't exist any more, Mr Vishwanath. They destroyed it in the revolution. I read about it in a book. Did you know about that?'

Mr Vishwanath nodded.

'Did you know about the lamp?' asked Amelia, hoping strongly that he hadn't.

'No,' said Mr Vishwanath. 'I didn't know about the lamp.'

Amelia smiled.

'The palace is not destroyed,' murmured Mr Vishwanath.

'Yes it is,' said Amelia. 'I read about it, Mr Vishwanath. And the Princess's driver, Asha, he said so as well.'

'Yes,' said Mr Vishwanath. 'It is destroyed materially, but nonetheless it still exists.'

'Where?' asked Amelia.

Mr Vishwanath turned to her. Suddenly the answer

came into Amelia's mind, and it seemed as if it arrived directly out of Mr Vishwanath's soft, dark eyes, as if he had somehow sent it into her head.

'In the Princess's mind,' whispered Amelia. 'That's where it still exists, isn't it?'

Mr Vishwanath turned away and gazed at the garden again.

Amelia frowned. She wasn't sure she understood herself what she had just said. The thought had suddenly been there and the words just came out of her mouth. In fact, she wasn't sure that she understood anything more now than she had before she sat down to speak with Mr Vishwanath, and possibly less.

'I think I'm still confused, Mr Vishwanath.'

Mr Vishwanath nodded.

'Is that a bad thing?'

Mr Vishwanath shrugged. 'It is what it is.'

Somehow, Amelia knew he was going to say that.

After a while, it began to make sense. Sort of. Amelia remembered something else Mr Vishwanath had told her. It was the Princess's tragedy that she lived her life worrying about whether people were treating her with enough importance. The two things fitted together. It was as if the Princess still lived in the palace, in her mind, and in her mind she was still as important a person as she had been when she really did live there.

In her mind, that life, which had come to an end with the revolution fifty-nine years ago, had never finished. And that would be a tragedy, wouldn't it, just as Mr Vishwanath said? It would be a tragedy if you were living a life in your mind that no longer existed. It would be like believing you were locked in a prison, and living your life as if you were – never stepping beyond the door of your cell, never gazing upwards to see the sky – except that there actually was no prison, and no cell in which you were locked, and no roof to block out the sky, but only imaginary bars and locks and walls which penned you in when all you had to do was step beyond them to be free.

And yet once you realised that, once you knew this imprisonment existed only in your mind . . . at that very moment, you would be released!

'It's so simple,' murmured Amelia to the sculpted lady as she stared out the window over Marburg Street. It was exactly as she had said to Mr Vishwanath when he first told her about the Princess's view of her life. 'The problem starts when you think it's complicated. But it's not. She just has to see how things look from the other side. Someone just has to tell her.'

Amelia glanced at the carved lady outside her window, and from the expression on the lady's face it definitely looked as if she agreed.

But what to do about it? Amelia didn't like the Princess, and the Princess had done nothing to make Amelia want to help her. And yet, when she had watched the Princess gazing at the lamp, when she had seen the tears glistening in her eyes, Amelia had got a glimpse of the part of the Princess that might not be so horrible, but might be tender, might be warm, like any other person. Maybe that would be the princess who would walk out of the prison once the Princess realised the prison was purely in her mind. And Amelia couldn't *not* try to help that princess, the tender one, the warm one, who had been imprisoned for fifty-nine years. She couldn't leave her there when it was such a simple thing to set her free. Because if not Amelia, who else would help her?

She glanced at the sculpted lady, and the sculpted lady was almost smiling in encouragement.

The next time the cream-coloured car came down the street, Amelia was ready. She knew exactly what she was going to say. She ran down the stairs. She was outside even before Asha had opened the door for the Princess. She waited excitedly for the Princess to get out.

'Princess!' she cried. 'Prince—'

Amelia stopped. The Princess had turned her gaze on her.

'You must say Your Serenity,' whispered Asha.

But Amelia didn't say anything. The gaze in the eyes of the Princess was one of pure ice. It gripped Amelia in its cold, bitter harshness, froze her blood. She felt as if, to the Princess, she was some kind of *thing* – not a person, not even an animal, but even less than that, some kind of fungus, perhaps – that was getting in the way.

The words she had prepared – the things she was going to say to show the Princess how simple the problem was – choked in Amelia's throat. Suddenly she felt ridiculously foolish, as she had felt when the Princess had called her story a fancy, a stupid, stupid thing. Worse, much worse. With that one freezing look, more powerful than a thousand words, the Princess had brought her back to reality. How could she, Amelia Dee, persuade someone like the Princess Parvin Kha-Douri to think about her life differently? It was absurd. What could she possibly say that the Princess hadn't heard before? How could she possibly imagine that the Princess would ever listen to her? The Princess would never change, nothing could ever make her see things afresh.

Everything that had seemed so simple in Amelia's room above the street now seemed impossibly complicated. Amelia felt as small as a bug, as if the Princess, if she chose to, could have taken two steps across and squashed her with her toe.

The Princess held her with her gaze a moment longer, then, as if knowing she had utterly crushed her, turned and went into Mr Vishwanath's studio.

Amelia was still frozen in her wake.

'Mademoiselle,' said the driver tentatively.

Amelia looked around. Still in a daze.

'Mademoiselle, you must understand—'

But Amelia couldn't bear to stay there a moment longer. Suddenly she just wanted to get away. She turned and ran inside.

So Amelia didn't hear what Asha was about to say. And Asha himself – who normally spoke not one word about his mistress, as a faithful servant mustn't – didn't know how much he might have revealed to the girl who had stared at him with such an injured, confused gaze on that pavement, had she not run off.

Because there was much that he could have said to Amelia. That already she had had an effect on his mistress, the Princess. That even the Princess Parvin Kha-Douri, who seemed outwardly so cold and severe, sometimes felt doubt. That she was at her most harsh with others when she doubted herself most deeply. And that he had never, in all the years he had spent with her, known her to be more harsh than in the days that had passed since she went into in the green house and saw the peacock lamp of her childhood hanging above the stairs.

CHAPTER 16

Amelia was angrier than she had ever been in her life. She sat in her room, almost trembling with rage. What right did the Princess have to treat her like that, to look at her as if she were no better than a dog? Not once, but twice. This was the second time! And why hadn't she said anything in response? She hated herself for that. Why had she stood there, dumb, shocked, instead of fighting back? She didn't know who she was angrier at, the Princess, or herself.

Why had Mr Vishwanath introduced her to the Princess in the first place? Why did he agree to teach yoga to such a cold, cruel woman? Wasn't he always saying he would rather have one true student than a hundred followers? He sent other people away but let the Princess keep coming. What kind of a true student was a person like that?

Amelia didn't know *what* to do, she was so angry and confused. If she didn't do something, it felt as if something inside her was going to snap.

She got up. She looked down at the street. There, directly below her, that was where it had happened.

The car was still there. Right now, the Princess would be in the studio on the ground floor, in her green leotard, with one foot hooked around her neck, probably. Amelia thought of going down and bursting in and knocking her off her one foot while the other was still hooked there.

A pigeon flew past. It looped up and landed on the head of the carved lady. It looked at Amelia. Its eye was red. It had an angry, aggressive look. Amelia watched it. The pigeon kept sitting there. Suddenly it took off and flapped away. Amelia could feel the wind from its wings as it went past.

'How can you bear that?' she demanded. 'The way they come and sit on you? Don't you hate it?'

The carved lady kept staring down at the street with her pupil-less eyes. Her face looked blank, silly, weak. Perfectly unperturbed.

'You should!' said Amelia. What was wrong with the carved lady? She ought to hate the way the pigeons came and sat on her. They'd been doing it for a hundred years. She ought to be angry. She ought to be as angry as anything.

Amelia looked down at the people on the street. She felt impatient with everyone. She could see the roofs of all the houses and shops on Marburg Street and of the houses in the streets beyond. You could see over everything from the top of the green house. If the

Princess lived in Marburg Street, thought Amelia, this was certainly where she'd want to live. But even this wouldn't be good enough for her. Nothing was good enough for her.

Amelia wondered how she could ever have imagined there was some good, gentle part of the Princess waiting to be released. What an idiot she had been! It was Mr Vishwanath's fault. He had put the idea in her head. Inside everyone, he had said, there is beauty. Wrong! Inside the Princess there was nothing but more of what there was on the outside. Self-importance and bitterness. Bitterness, especially bitterness.

Amelia had never met anyone else as bitter. Not even close. Compare the Princess with Mr Chan, Kevin's cousin, who had lost a leg in some kind of accident in the factory where he worked. Amelia couldn't quite understand how Mr Chan could be Kevin's cousin, because he was about fifty years old, but apparently he was, and ever since the accident he had had to walk with an artificial leg. The artificial leg had a brown shoe on its artificial foot, and Mr Chan couldn't wear anything but brown shoes on his real foot so they'd match. He couldn't work any more because of his accident. But he wasn't bitter. In fact, he was one of the most cheerful people Amelia knew, always laughing. He grew vegetables in his backyard, but he didn't call it his backyard, he called it his farm, and chuckled when he said it. His farm was about five metres long! And every little patch of vegetables – carrots, broccoli, whatever – wasn't a patch, it was a field.

Mr Chan wasn't bitter, and he had more of a right to be bitter than the Princess. Surely it was worse to lose your leg than your palace.

'At least you can still walk after you've lost your palace,' muttered Amelia. 'At least you can wear any shoe you like, and it doesn't have to be brown!'

Amelia looked at the carved lady to see what she had to say to that. But the carved lady looked back at her blankly, as if she wouldn't even know how to begin.

Amelia rolled her eyes. 'Put a pigeon on your head!' she said, and she turned away from the window.

She threw herself down in her chair. Her pen was on the desk in front of her. She hadn't written a thing since the Princess told her how stupid her story was.

She picked up the pen now, absent-mindedly, still fuming.

Bitter, she thought. Bitter bitter bitter.

She grabbed a piece of paper. She wrote.

The Bitter Princess

She looked at the words. Impulsively, she put her pen to the paper again.

There was once a princess who was extremely bitter. She wasn't a young, beautiful princess, like you read about in fairy tales, she was old and wrinkled. This wasn't because of a spell that some horrible witch had cast on her, like you would find in a fairy tale. It was because of a spell she had cast on herself.

That was right. A spell she had cast on herself! It was her own fault she was bitter. It was her own fault she couldn't think about anything but the things she had lost.

It wasn't an old-fashioned magic spell like the kind you would find in a fairy tale. It was a modern kind of spell, and it meant the Princess could only think of everything she had lost. Every day, that's what she thought about, everything she had lost. She never thought about all the things she still had.

Amelia paused. She was starting to get interested in the story now, where it would go, how it would develop. How had the spell come to be cast? After all, why would anyone cast a spell over herself? Amelia thought about it. Maybe it had happened without her knowing.

The spell was cast when the Princess was only a little girl. One night, very late, when she was asleep in her grand palace, her servant came running in and woke her up. There was an angry crowd outside, and they only had minutes to escape.

And? Amelia considered. What now? Maybe, if you were a certain age, if were woken at a certain time, when the moon was full and the night was black, then you would be bitter for the rest of your life. Maybe in everyone's life there was one particular moment like that, and if you happened to be woken at that moment – and it happened very rarely, because the chances were low – then you would be bitter for as long as you lived. And maybe the opposite was true as well, there was a moment which would make you cheerful for the rest of your life, like Mr Chan, even if terrible things happened to you.

Now, it just so happened that at the moment the Princess was woken the moon was full and the night was black. There is a moment like this in everybody's life. Most of us sleep through it, and wake up safely the next morning. But if you are woken up at that exact moment, as the Princess was that night when the crowd had come to burn the palace

Amelia stopped. This was wrong. If that was how the spell was cast, it wasn't the Princess's fault. She could never stop being bitter, because she happened to be woken up at the wrong moment, and once that happened, she was doomed. But the Princess had to have some control if it was going to be her own fault. She had to be the one who cast the spell on herself –

143

maybe not intentionally, but she still had to be the one who cast it.

Amelia scratched out the last lines, everything she had written since she wrote that the princess had only minutes to escape. She thought. How would a person cast a spell on herself unintentionally, yet still be responsible for it? Maybe . . . maybe because of what she was like. Could that be it? Because of something about her, or the way she behaved. Because she was so awful, or thoughtless, or disobedient, or spoiled, and wouldn't listen to anybody else.

Amelia nodded. Now she had it.

All around there was noise, and shouting, and the Princess, who was hardly awake, didn't know what was happening. The servant picked her up and carried her away. 'Don't look!' said the servant, and he held her close, risking his own life to save her. But the Princess squirmed and wriggled and managed to peek over his shoulder. 'Don't look!' cried the servant again, 'these are things you must not see.' But the Princess shouted back at him, 'Don't tell me what to do! You're just a servant!' She was a thoughtless girl, and very uppity, and she thought she was better than all her servants, and she never thanked them when they did things for her. She was spoiled, even for a princess, and never did anything her servants said, always thinking she knew better. And it was the same on this night, and she didn't even care that the poor servant was risking his life to save her. She wriggled and squirmed in his arms until she could see again. Every time the servant told her to look away, she shouted back, and every time he tried to press her close, she squirmed and screamed until she could see. And in her eyes, the palace burned. The flames rose high into the darkness of the night, destroying all the things the Princess had and all the other things she would have had. She wouldn't take her eyes off it, not for a second, even though the servant kept telling her to. That was how the spell was cast. From that night on, she could only think about the things she had lost when the palace burned. And she had only herself to blame, because if she had only done as she was told for once in her life, if she hadn't been so thoughtless and disobedient, it never would have happened.

Amelia looked back over what she had written. Perfect. Now, where was the story going next? Her teacher was always saying you had to plan your stories before you started writing, but Amelia rarely did that. Not for the stories she wrote for herself, anyway. She liked to see where they went by themselves. That was the thing Amelia loved most about writing. You never knew what ideas or characters were going to come out, and if you were lucky, you found that something very clever, or funny, or scary, had appeared. So it must have been inside you all along, but you wouldn't have known if you hadn't written the story in the first place, or if you had tried to plan it too carefully before you started. But that did mean sometimes you got a bit stuck. Especially when it came to the ending. Endings could be tricky when you hadn't planned anything about your story.

But not this time. Amelia soon knew what to write next, and the story ran on. She covered both sides of the first page, and went on to a second, then a third. The Princess was older now. She was in a new country. She met new people. Some of them wanted to be her friends, but she rejected them, thinking of the friends she might have had if she hadn't been forced to flee her home. When she had grown up, a handsome, clever man wanted to marry her, but she refused, thinking of the princes who might have wanted to marry her had her parents still ruled her country. An hour later, Amelia had covered almost a dozen pages. The Princess was old, lonely and unhappy, and her only companion was the ancient servant who had woken her on that fateful night. Finally, her servant died, and a month later, the Princess died as well, utterly alone, utterly forgotten, with only her bitterness to keep her company at the end. And when they found her body locked in her room, years later, it was just a skeleton, and no one had any idea who she had been.

Amelia put down her pen.

She glanced over the story, flipping through the pages. In many ways, it was a horrible story, more horrible than the so-called horror stories she liked to read. It wasn't exactly bloodcurdling, there were no vampires or murderers or bloodstained knives. And it wasn't about something an evil person does to other people, which is what most horror stories were about. It was about something evil a person does to herself. But that, Amelia realised, was what made it all the more horrible.

Good, she thought.

CHAPTER 17

The story lay in the drawer in Amelia's desk, together with other stories she had written. But it wasn't the same as the other stories. There was something strange about it. Amelia didn't look at the story after she had put it away, not even once, didn't even dare to open the drawer. Yet she could feel it there, almost as if it was a living, breathing thing, almost as if it needed to be heard and couldn't be locked away in a dark drawer and forgotten. Almost as if it was waiting to get out.

Amelia didn't know what to do with it. Sometimes she wanted to grab the story out of the drawer and tear it up, and sometimes she wanted to thrust it at the Princess and make her read it. Yet somehow Amelia couldn't bring herself to do either.

And in the meantime, every few days, the cream-coloured car came up Marburg Street and stopped in front of the green house. The Princess got out and went into Mr Vishwanath's studio for her yoga lesson, just as she always had. The story continued to lie in the drawer, waiting to come out, and there was no time that Amelia was more strongly conscious of it than when she saw the cream-coloured car pulling up in the street under her window.

Other strange things were happening. As time passed, Eugenie talked about her meeting with the Princess in a way that didn't match what had actually occurred. At first she told people she had met a princess, because she wanted people to know. She didn't say what this 'meeting' consisted of. Then she began to say the Princess had smiled at her, and then she began to say the Princess had said 'Good afternoon' to her, and then she began to say that the Princess had talked to her, and in the end she was describing a whole conversation between herself and the Princess that had never taken place. At least, Amelia couldn't remember it taking place. Neither could Kevin. Eugenie was lying.

'I'm not lying!' retorted Eugenie, after Amelia had heard her describe the latest version of the meeting to someone else.

'Eugenie,' said Amelia, 'the Princess never asked you to come for tea.'

'Of course she did. Don't you remember?'

'No, I don't remember,' said Amelia.

'Well, you've forgotten,' said Eugenie.

'Eugenie, I haven't forgotten. She never said such a thing. If she did, why haven't you been to tea with her?'

'She said she'd let me know when she was available.'

'Then why hasn't she let you know?'

Eugenie laughed, as if that was the simplest question in the world. 'She's busy. She's a princess! It'll probably be a year until she has time.'

'Eugenie, the Princess never said that to you. None of it. You know she didn't.'

'Of course she did. She said: "It was lovely to meet you, Mademoiselle Eugenie, and you must come and take tea. I'll let you know when it's convenient."'

Amelia stared at Eugenie. The words had come out so easily, so confidently, it would be easy to believe that the Princess really had said them. And Eugenie was looking at Amelia so openly, so unashamedly, it was hard to believe she was consciously lying. So hard to believe, in fact, that Amelia found herself asking Kevin whether the version that Eugenie was telling – or something like it, at least – hadn't actually happened.

Kevin looked at Amelia incredulously.

'You don't think . . .' Amelia frowned. 'We couldn't have missed it, could we? The Princess couldn't have said those things to Eugenie while we weren't looking?'

Kevin rolled his eyes. 'Amelia, even if the Princess wanted to talk to her, she couldn't have. Eugenie didn't stop curtsying. Even when we went inside she kept curtsying. She's lying, Amelia. You know Eugenie. She'll say anything to make herself seem important.'

But Eugenie wasn't lying, that was what Amelia began to understand. Not in the sense of someone who says something false while consciously knowing it's untrue. Somehow, Eugenie had actually come to believe what she was saying. Amelia realised that Eugenie genuinely no longer knew what was reality and what was her imagination. Or to put it another way, Eugenie's imagination had become her reality. So strongly did she wish that the Princess had said those things to her, she had come to believe the Princess actually had said them. Eugenie had created a kind of myth of what had happened that day, and now she was turning that myth into the truth.

And Kevin, in a way, was doing the same thing. Eugenie hadn't kept curtsying when they went inside, Amelia was sure of it. Wasn't she?

Amelia found this very strange, and perplexing. And interesting. Who was to say Eugenie was wrong? Only Amelia and Kevin had been there with her throughout the entire encounter. And if Amelia or Kevin were to tell a different version, why should anyone believe them rather than Eugenie? After all, Amelia had found herself wondering whether Eugenie wasn't right, so convincing and genuine did she seem. Amelia found it quite extraordinary, the way a myth that someone created could make you doubt what you yourself knew to be true. But how *did* you know it was true? And if Eugenie could do it, how often must other, cleverer people do it? It made Amelia wonder about a lot of things. About the things she learned in history, for example. How could she be sure any of it was true, and that one part or another wasn't just some kind of myth that someone had invented and which everyone had started to believe, blotting out the memory of what had really happened? Especially where one side were winners, for example, and the other side were losers, and only the winners got to tell their side of the story.

Amelia glanced out the window at the carved lady. Suddenly Amelia felt as if she were floating, completely disconnected, and everything around her was just a kind of illusion. *Nothing* was certain. How did she know the world itself even existed and wasn't just something inside her own imagination? Maybe she was asleep, and this whole life she thought she was living was just a dream. And the dreams she had at night, they were dreams within a dream. So nothing really existed, not the carved lady she could supposedly see outside her window, nor the lamp at the top of the stairs outside her room, nor the green house that contained the stairs, nor the people who lived in the house, her mother or her father or Mrs Ellis or Mr Vishwanath or she, Amelia Dee. Although Amelia must exist, because everything was inside her imagination. But who could tell who Amelia really was? Maybe a boy called Edward. Or an old lady called Phyllis. Or a snail with an exceptionally active mind.

Mrs Ellis had no doubt that she existed. 'Amelia Dee!' she exclaimed, when Amelia tried out the idea on her. 'What *are* you talking about? I don't know where you get these ideas, I really don't.' She tasted the soup she was making, took a pinch of salt, and sprinkled it into the pot.

'Don't you ever wonder?' asked Amelia.

'I haven't time to wonder!' replied Mrs Ellis. 'The hall wants sweeping yet. Do you think it's going to sweep itself?'

'No,' said Amelia. Then she thought about that. If the whole world was only happening inside her imagination, maybe she *could* imagine a hall that would sweep itself.

'What are you doing now?' demanded Mrs Ellis.

'Just thinking,' said Amelia.

Mrs Ellis looked at her suspiciously, as if wondering whether she should ask what Amelia had been thinking about. She decided not to. Amelia wondered whether she should tell her anyway. But only for a minute.

She went into the hall. She tried to imagine it into a hall that would sweep itself, whatever that might look like. She gazed fiercely at the floor, imagining as hard as she could. But it didn't happen. The hall remained determinedly non-sweeping – until Mrs Ellis bustled in with her broom. But that wasn't exactly what Amelia had meant.

Amelia went out to the garden. Maybe the fact that she hadn't been able to imagine the hall into something that was self-sweeping – even though Amelia wasn't aware of any kind of floor in the whole world that was capable of sweeping itself – proved that the world wasn't just in her imagination. If it *was* in her imagination, surely she would be able to turn the floor of the hall into anything she wanted.

Outside, she found Mr Vishwanath sitting in his chair. She sat down beside him.

'What do you think, Mr Vishwanath? If I can't make the hall self-sweeping, does that prove the world really exists?'

Mr Vishwanath looked at her, not in surprise, but as if it was the most normal question in the world, one he had heard any number of times before, and he understood exactly why Amelia was asking it.

'Maybe the powers of your mind are not powerful enough,' he replied.

'Oh.' Amelia frowned. She hadn't thought about that possibility. Maybe the whole world really was just a thing inside her imagination, but her imagination wasn't powerful enough to make it exactly as she wanted it to be. That would explain why so many things happened that she would have preferred not to have happened. 'Is your mind powerful enough?' she said to Mr Vishwanath.

'If the whole world is inside your mind, my mind is inside there as well,' he replied.

Amelia's eyes narrowed. That would mean right now she was talking to herself. It was tricky, when you started thinking about stuff like this. 'Your mind can't be stronger, then, can it?' she said cautiously. 'It can't be stronger than mine, if it's part of mine.'

'Maybe it contains some of the powers of your mind that you are not consciously aware of,' said Mr Vishwanath. 'Maybe your mind has put them there, as if they are outside yourself, because you do not want to acknowledge that they are yours.'

Amelia frowned again. This was getting *really* tricky. What if that was what her mind had done, and Mr Vishwanath was just some kind of illusory embodiment of a part of her mind that the rest of her mind didn't want to acknowledge? But why on earth would her mind embody it as an old yoga master who liked to stand for hours in a blue nappy with one foot hooked around his neck? Who was so cautious and private that he wouldn't even put up an advertisement in his studio window? Who was always saying he had been such a wild character – but only in his youth?

'What do you think, Mr Vishwanath?' asked Amelia eventually.

'What does it matter what I think, if I don't really exist?' Mr Vishwanath gazed at Amelia for a moment, and then smiled his gentle, probing smile. He turned back and looked at the garden again.

Amelia watched him. If nothing really existed outside her mind, then Mr Vishwanath didn't exist outside her mind, and if Mr Vishwanath didn't exist outside her mind, then all the things he said didn't exist outside her mind either. Which meant they were already in her mind. Which meant *she* was the one who was really saying them. But she couldn't be the one saying them, because she hardly ever understood them!

In Amelia's opinion, that was the strongest proof that the world really *did* exist. Much stronger than her failure to turn the hall into a self-sweeping floor.

'You really do exist, Mr Vishwanath,' she said.

Mr Vishwanath glanced at her for a moment, and then turned back to the garden.

There was silence.

The garden seemed empty without any statues. They were all stacked down the back, behind the invention shed. Amelia's father was waiting for the first sculpture from her mother's new phase. He was certain it wouldn't be long now before the door of the sculpture room opened to reveal a new work. He said it as if he was quite excited about it.

The thought reminded Amelia of her story again, still sitting in her drawer, waiting to come out.

Amelia frowned. None of her stories had ever given her this kind of trouble. Normally she wrote them and put them away and that was that. Something might make her think of one of them, and she might pull it out and read it again, but only for her own entertainment. But this one just wouldn't rest. It made her wonder why she had written it in the first place. For that matter, why did she write any of her stories? She had never really stopped to think about it. But why? What was the point of writing something that just sat in a drawer for ever? That was as bad as . . . as bad as what her mother did with her sculptures, putting them in the garden and never letting anyone see them.

But what was the story for? Did she really want the Princess to read it, even if she could make her?

There was no one she could ask. No one knew she had ever written a single story, except the Princess. And Mr Vishwanath. She had told him, Amelia remembered.

She looked at him now. She could smell the sweet scent of his yoga oil. He was gazing at the garden, perfectly still. There was no way of knowing what was going on in his mind.

'Mr Vishwanath?'

Mr Vishwanath went on gazing ahead.

Amelia hesitated. 'I wrote a story,' she said softly.

'Another one?' murmured Mr Vishwanath, in that

tone of his, so deep, so gentle, you never knew if it wasn't coming from inside your own head.

'I can't decide what to do with it.'

There was a chirruping from somewhere in the grass. A cricket.

'What makes you think you should do anything with it?' said Mr Vishwanath, still gazing at the garden.

'I don't know. I just can't leave it. I can't explain why.'

'What have you thought you might do with it?'

Amelia hesitated. 'Give it to the Princess.'

There was silence.

'Mr Vishwanath, I was thinking ... maybe you could read it.'

Just before five o'clock the next afternoon, the hammering and banging in the sculpture room stopped. Not just for a minute or two, but completely. Suddenly, for the first time in weeks, there was silence.

Amelia knew what that meant. She came down from her room. Her father came in from the invention shed. They met on the landing on the second floor.

Another few minutes went by. Then Amelia's mother flung open the door. But instead of coming out and quickly locking it behind her, she stepped back and waited impatiently inside.

In the middle of the room, in a mess of fragments of plaster and wood shavings and metal scraps, stood a sculpture. It was about two metres high, and a metre wide, all green-yellow metal. There was a big, undulating metal ring at the top, and a metal ring at the bottom, and a set of metal struts that ran between them all curling and curving and crossing over each other. It was like a kind of tube that had been twisted and squeezed and then lengthened again.

Amelia's father stared at it. Then he glanced at the hoist in the window of the sculpture room, and back at the sculpture, and his expression grew more and more worried.

Amelia's mother was gazing at it as well, head cocked, a slight frown on her face, as if she was seeing it for the very first time. Then she looked at Amelia.

'Well?' she said.

Amelia nodded. Always nod, she had learned from her father. Nod thoughtfully, slowly, and preferably a number of times, as if you approved wholeheartedly of whatever you were seeing. Even if you had no idea what it was.

Her mother glanced questioningly at her father.

He nodded as well, exactly the same kind of slow, thoughtful, methodical nod.

This was going to be tricky, thought Amelia. There was only one person who could get them out of the situation, one person blunt enough and brusque enough to ask the question no one else dared to ask.

'What in the world is that?'

Amelia and her father glanced at each other in relief. Mrs Ellis was standing behind them in the doorway, hands on hips, with a look of disbelief on her face.

'It's a lamp,' snapped Amelia's mother.

'A lamp?' Mrs Ellis hooted with laughter. 'What good is a lamp like that? How do you light it?'

'You don't light it,' snapped Amelia's mother.

'Oh, a lamp you don't light!' Mrs Ellis hooted again. 'What's it for, then?'

'It's not *for* anything,' snapped Amelia's mother. 'It's an interpretation of a lamp.' She turned around and ignored the housekeeper.

But Mrs Ellis wasn't to be ignored. She took a couple of steps into the room and waved her arm at all the rubbish on the floor. 'Well, don't expect me to clear all this up for you. You can do it yourself!'

Mrs Ellis always said that. Amelia's mother's reply, which was always the same, came quickly.

'You'll clear it up, Mrs Ellis! You'll clear it up if I tell you to clear it up.'

'I will not!'

'You will so!'

'I will *not*!'

'You will *so*! You'll clear it up right now!'

'Just see if I do,' retorted Mrs Ellis, and she turned on her heel and left the room.

She wouldn't clear it up right now. She'd come back in a couple of hours. That way, they could both claim to have won. Amelia's mother would have forced Mrs Ellis to clear up the mess after Mrs Ellis had refused. And Mrs Ellis would have done it when she chose after she had been told to do it straight away. On the other hand, thought Amelia, if you looked at it another way, each of them could be said to have lost . . .

'So it's a lamp,' said Amelia's father.

'Of course, it's a lamp,' snapped Amelia's mother. 'I hardly need to tell you that, Armand.'

'Of course you don't, Angeline. I was just confirming my impression. That was your impression, wasn't it, Amelia?'

'Definitely.'

'An interpretation of a lamp,' said Amelia's father.

'Yes,' said her mother.

Amelia's father nodded. 'And you don't plan to light it?' he asked, as if to reassure himself.

'Of course I don't intend to light it!' retorted Amelia's mother. 'Honestly! What's wrong with you today, Armand? I've enough to put up with from Mrs Ellis!'

Amelia's father smiled understandingly. Amelia's mother was always touchy after she had just finished a sculpture, particularly the first sculpture of a new phase. Artists were like that, he often said to Amelia. Inventors weren't, he always added. At least he wasn't. He was always cheerful, even when one of his inventions had just failed miserably. But Amelia thought that was because most of his inventions failed miserably, and if he couldn't be cheerful when that happened, he would hardly ever be cheerful at all.

He walked slowly around the sculpture, considering it from every angle. Amelia's mother watched him anxiously.

'Well, I think it's wonderful,' he said at last.

'Do you, Armand?' Amelia's mother beamed. 'Really?'

'Of course I do, my love.' Amelia's father came back and kissed her. Then he put his arm around her waist, and they stood side by side, gazing at the sculpture.

'What about you, Amelia?' asked Amelia's mother, and she reached for her hand.

'Oh, I love it as well,' said Amelia.

'Really?' said her mother. 'What do you most love about it?'

Amelia stared. 'Well . . . I love the . . . the . . .'

'Do you love the torsion in the shape?' she said.

'Yes! Yes, I do.'

'Yes, the torsion,' said her father. 'We both love the torsion, don't we, Amelia?'

Amelia nodded.

'I wasn't sure about it at first,' said her mother. 'Yet it felt necessary. It felt right.'

'I can see what you mean,' said her father, cocking his head. 'And tell me, Angelica, is this the start of a new phase, or a one-off?'

'Neither,' replied Amelia's mother. 'It's the first of a series.'

'A series?' said Amelia's father. 'And the difference between a series and a phase . . . that would be . . .?'

'Honestly, Armand! What *is* wrong with you today? A phase is open-ended. Who knows how long it will go for? A series is defined. It has a goal. It has a limit.'

Amelia's father nodded seriously. 'A series. Perfect. Yes, Amelia? We haven't had a series before, have we?'

Amelia shook her head.

'I thought I'd do six.'

'Six?'

'Yes. Six different interpretations. I got the idea from that princess. What if the six lamps in the palace weren't the same type, but each one was a completely different style? And what if each one was . . . Well, look at the one we've got hanging at the top of the stairs. It's beautiful in its own way, I won't deny it. But it's very old-fashioned. Very classical. What if you had six that were completely different but modern? That's what I wanted to do. Make a new interpretation.'

Amelia's father gave his wife a kiss. 'Always thinking like that, aren't you, Angelita? Always looking for something original. I'd never have thought of it.'

'Nonsense, Armando,' said Amelia's mother, and she caressed her husband's cheek. 'You're the one who's always thinking of new things.' But she couldn't keep the smile off her face, and anyone could see how pleased she was at what Amelia's father had said.

Amelia rolled her eyes.

Her father got the lamp into the garden using the sculpture hoist. It creaked and wobbled, but held the weight, and the lamp eventually made it down safely. He positioned it in the garden under the watchful eye of Amelia's mother. Then Amelia's mother turned around and went inside.

'Do you think she's really going to make six?' said Amelia.

Her father shrugged. They both looked at the garden, trying to visualise what it would look like with six lamp interpretations in it.

'Do you like it?' asked Amelia. 'Really?'

Her father gazed at the sculpture, then he walked around a little way and gazed at it from a different angle.

'Well?'

'That's not the point,' he said.

Amelia knew what was coming next.

'Your mother expressed herself, that's the only thing that matters.'

Of course that was the only thing that mattered, thought Amelia, if you only put your sculptures in your backyard where no one else would ever see them. But just once in a while, would it really hurt if her mother expressed herself in a way that other people actually liked?

'You know,' said her father, gazing at it again, 'I think I actually do like it. It's the . . . the . . .'

'Torsion?'

Her father shook his head, trying to look at Amelia disapprovingly. But he couldn't quite keep a smile off his lips. Then he became thoughtful again. 'No, but really, there is something interesting about it. It might be quite interesting to have six of them here.' He looked around the garden, as if he could already see them there. 'Yes, it might be quite interesting.'

Amelia shrugged. The sculpture wasn't so bad. Better than the horrible thin face-blades that had been there before. Maybe it really was because of the torsion, whatever that was.

'Maybe we *could* light them. What do you think?'

Amelia looked at her father. Was he serious?

'Still,' he said, 'that Princess of yours – I probably wouldn't show them to her. She didn't look like the type who'd approve.'

'Of anything,' muttered Amelia.

They glanced at each other and shared a smile.

'Do you know that Eugenie Edelstein thinks the Princess had a whole conversation with her?' said Amelia.

'I didn't hear her say anything to Eugenie.'

'No,' said Amelia. 'No one did but Eugenie.'

'She had a rather interesting conversation with your mother, though, didn't she?'

Amelia stared at him. 'When?'

'When your mother came out of the sculpture room. About what she did. About her art.'

'No, she didn't. She just said . . .'

'What?' asked Amelia's father, with a look of genuine interest.

Amelia shook her head in disbelief. Did *everyone* recall only what they wanted to remember?

'What, Amelia?'

'Nothing.'

Amelia's father waited a moment longer. Then he laughed. He rubbed his hands together. 'Well, I've got work to do. I've had an excellent idea! The lamp's given it to me. It's about getting a flare to burn better underwater.'

'How would you light it?'

'Easy. It can already be done, that part isn't the problem.'

'But if it can already be done, why would you want to . . .' Amelia stopped. Her father was looking at her with an expression of intense interest, waiting for her to go on.

'What?' he said.

'Nothing,' said Amelia.

'If we didn't think about getting underwater flares to burn better, Amelia, we'd still be in the Stone Age.'

Amelia nodded.

Her father smiled, rubbing his hands together again. 'Right. Don't disturb me! I may be some time.'

He headed past the lamp to the invention shed at the end of the garden. Amelia watched him go. She didn't understand her father. Sometimes he seemed the most intelligent person she had ever met. But let him in sight of the invention shed, and you'd think he was completely insane.

The door of the shed closed behind him. Amelia looked at the lamp sculpture. It stood in the garden, tall, twisted, with grass poking through the gaps between its curving metal struts.

Amelia walked around it, considering it from the other side. Maybe you really could light it. Put a candle in the middle. Or a lantern. At night. There'd be shadows from the struts. Curving all over the garden walls and the back of the house. And from the undulating ring at the top. Its wavy shadow would run high up there . . .

Amelia saw her mother in the window of the sculpture room. She was beside the hoist, watching. Amelia smiled. Her mother smiled back, and disappeared.

Amelia looked at the sculpture again. She frowned.

Suddenly it seemed to Amelia that she had under-estimated her mother. She did show her sculptures to people. Maybe it was only to her husband, and her daughter, and her housekeeper, and the yoga master who lived on the ground floor, but maybe they were the only people whose opinions mattered to her. And so what if the sculptures never left the backyard? It was still something to put them there where at least some people could see them, it was still braver than leaving them in a drawer – or under a drape, or behind a screen, or whatever the equivalent for sculptures would be.

It was a lot braver than what Amelia had done with her story about the bitter princess. Even giving it to Mr Vishwanath, she knew, was a way of not taking a chance, getting someone to look at it privately before showing it to anyone else.

She regretted that now. Almost as soon as she had given the story to Mr Vishwanath, as soon as the pages left her hand, she had realised why she had left it hidden for so long before deciding to do even that. It wasn't a good story. She was ashamed of it. It was nasty and childish. The more she thought about it, the more she cringed.

And she had given it to Mr Vishwanath. Mr Vish-wanath, of all people! What would he think of her when he read it? She only hoped he'd lost it, or forgotten about it, or something, so he'd never see what she had written.

But he wouldn't have lost it, Amelia knew. And he wouldn't forget to do something once he had said he would, not Mr Vishwanath.

CHAPTER 19

Slowly, Mr Vishwanath's head turned. Amelia stopped. She had hoped she might slip past without him noticing. Although she couldn't keep trying to sneak around him forever.

'Hello, Mr Vishwanath,' she said.

'Hello Amelia.'

He continued to watch her. Expectantly. There was no point trying to put it off any longer. She went and sat beside him.

Mr Vishwanath turned back to look at the garden. Amelia stole a glance at him, wondering when he was going to say something. It would be almost a relief to get it over with.

But he was silent, staring at the sculpture.

'My mother says it's a new interpretation of the old,' said Amelia at last. 'Of the lamp. In our house.'

'So that's what it is.'

'It's the torsion,' said Amelia. 'Apparently that's the important bit.'

Mr Vishwanath nodded.

There was silence.

'What do you think about new interpretations of the old?' asked Amelia eventually.

'Many old things are the inspiration for the new,' said Mr Vishwanath. 'There is nothing strange about this. All through history, this has been the case.'

Amelia looked at him in surprise.

'What?' said Mr Vishwanath. 'Did you think I would oppose something just because it is new?'

'No,' said Amelia hurriedly.

'Yes, I think you did.'

'No . . . Yes. I did.'

'Why? If there is never any new interpretation, Amelia, we would stand still. Nothing would ever get any better.'

'We'd still be in the Stone Age?'

Mr Vishwanath smiled. 'If we were not prepared to create new interpretations, we would have nothing new to say. Our voices would be taken away by the generations that came before us, even before we had learned to use them.'

Amelia frowned. That would make a lot of people unhappy, if their voices were taken away. She could think of half a dozen without even trying, starting with a certain mythmaker called Eugenie Edelstein.

'The thing is . . .' said Amelia, 'I mean, I don't think the sculpture's necessarily that bad, I just think I like the original version of the lamp better.'

'Not every new interpretation is an improvement,' murmured Mr Vishwanath. He glanced at the sculpture standing in the garden, and then he looked back at Amelia, with just a twinkle of a smile in his eyes.

Amelia laughed.

'Still,' said Mr Vishwanath, 'that doesn't mean we shouldn't try. In some cases, ways that are new may be good.'

'Then what about advertising for students, Mr Vish—'

'But in other cases,' continued Mr Vishwanath solemnly, 'the ways that are old are better.'

Amelia sighed. 'Well, the original lamp is so beautiful, Mr Vishwanath, I don't think you could ever improve on it.'

'Perhaps,' said Mr Vishwanath. 'Still, your mother has not done a bad job.'

'There are five more to come! And every one of them is going to be different.'

Mr Vishwanath didn't reply, but Amelia thought she saw one of his eyebrows rise. Just slightly.

There was silence again. Amelia didn't feel awkward any more, as she had when she first sat down. Perhaps Mr Vishwanath hadn't read the story, after all.

'I think I can understand why the Princess feels like she does,' said Amelia, gazing at the sculpture. 'Not just because of the lamp. That's only one example. Her whole life was perfect.'

'No one's life is perfect,' said Mr Vishwanath.

'True, but that's probably how it seems to her. Her life was perfect, just like the lamp. You couldn't improve on it. And then it was gone. Like the lamp. She loved the lamp, and all of sudden, it's gone. Forever.'

'Gone from her,' said Mr Vishwanath. 'But not gone. Someone else enjoys its beauty. Now it's you who loves the lamp.'

'But that doesn't help her.'

'It inspired your mother also,' said Mr Vishwanath. 'That's another thing. By inspiring your mother, it gave her something very precious.'

Amelia remembered the look on her mother's face when her father said he liked the sculpture. 'Yes, that's true. But the Princess doesn't know about that. And even if she knew, she wouldn't care.'

Mr Vishwanath was silent. He got up. He held up a finger, to tell Amelia to wait, and went inside. When he came out again, he was carrying a sheaf of pages.

Amelia's heart sank.

'You really don't need to worry about that, Mr Vishwanath.' Amelia forced a laugh. 'It was silly. I'm sure you didn't waste your time reading it, did you? I don't know why I even gave it to you. It was just a . . . just a . . .'

Mr Vishwanath held out the pages.

Amelia took them. 'What did you think?' she asked softly.

'I do not think you should give it to the Princess.'

Amelia nodded. 'It's not very good, is it?'

'I am not a judge of writing,' said Mr Vishwanath. 'I cannot say if it is good or bad. But I think it is a story you wrote out of anger. Maybe it's a story you wrote as a kind of revenge because you didn't like the Princess or the way she treated you.'

'I *didn't* like the way she treated me, if you want to know the truth. Or Kevin. Or Eugenie. Although you wouldn't know it,' added Amelia in exasperation, 'not if you hear Eugenie tell the story.'

Mr Vishwanath didn't reply.

Amelia frowned. She sat back in her chair and folded her arms. She was angry again, but this time at herself. She was so embarrassed. Mr Vishwanath was right. She had written the story as a kind of revenge. But what kind of a revenge was that? It was pathetic.

'Amelia?'

She couldn't bear to look at him. She couldn't imagine what he must think of her.

'Amelia, it is alright to have written it. We all get angry.'

Amelia glanced at him disbelievingly.

Mr Vishwanath smiled. 'When I was younger, I had quite a rage.'

Amelia shook her head. To listen to Mr Vishwanath, you'd think he was the wildest, most uncontrollable person ever. When he was younger.

Amelia shook her head again, eyes narrowed. 'I'm never going to show anyone one of my stories again. Never ever ever!'

Mr Vishwanath didn't reply.

'It never works! It's always a disaster! I'll leave it to Martin Martinez.'

'Who is Martin Martinez?'

'Doesn't matter.'

Mr Vishwanath nodded. 'Do you think your anger is gone? The anger you felt when you wrote this story?'

Amelia gazed at the pages in her hand. She sighed. 'Maybe,' she murmured.

'Then isn't there something better you can say to the Princess? Something that isn't written for revenge?'

'I told you, Mr Vishwanath, it doesn't matter. I'm never going to show anything to anyone again.'

Mr Vishwanath turned back to the garden. It was a moment before he spoke. 'I think, a girl who can write so wonderfully, isn't there something more wonderful that she can write? Not anger and revenge, but something with hope, maybe, and understanding.'

Amelia didn't reply.

'A girl who has the ability to make a story come alive in such a way. There must be a more beautiful story that she can tell, if she wants to.'

Amelia frowned. 'Mr Vishwanath,' she said quietly, 'I thought you said you're not a judge of writing.'

Mr Vishwanath shrugged. 'An amateur, at best.'

Mr Vishwanath got up and walked into the garden. He stopped beside the sculpture. He twisted himself around, and then twisted his arms around his twisted body, until he seemed like some kind of a human version of the twisted metal of the sculpture. Then he closed his eyes, and held the position.

Amelia stared at him. She hadn't seen him do that pose before. It was a new one. Amelia knew what it was. It was an interpretation of the sculpture. Which was an interpretation of the lamp. And elsewhere, in the invention shed, at that very moment, her father was working on an idea he had got from the sculpture, which in a way was *another* interpretation of it. Suddenly it seemed to Amelia that the lamp had some kind of power that had been unleashed, inspiring people in all kinds of ways. There was something wonderful about it – a sculpture, an invention, a yoga pose, all drawing on the same source. And yet none of this would have happened, no one would have been inspired and none of these things would have been created, if there hadn't been a revolution in Irafia and the Grand Palace of Ervahan hadn't been destroyed and the lamp hadn't been looted and sold from one person to another and ended up – somehow, through some chain of events that no one could remember any more – at the top of the stairs in the green house that Solomon Weiszacker had built on Marburg Street.

Amelia looked at the pages lying in her lap. The words that were on those pages, they weren't the story. This was. The real story wasn't about the Princess. It was about the lamp!

Amelia jumped up and ran inside.

In the garden, Mr Vishwanath opened one eye and watched her go.

CHAPTER 20

Amelia didn't hesitate for a second. As soon as she got back to her desk she pulled out a piece of paper. She picked up her pen. There are times – very few, very rare – when you know with complete, crystal clarity what you are trying to say, and the words find themselves. It seemed that they were on the page before Amelia had even consciously thought them. And it didn't matter that they were strange. She knew they were right, perfectly right.

I am a lamp.

Yes, thought Amelia. To be the lamp, that was the way to understand what had happened to the Princess. What had happened to her world. The lamp would tell.

I was made long ago by the most skilful lamp-maker in the ancient city of Ervahan. He made six of us, and when he had made us, he took us to the Grand Palace, and there we hung each one of us in a different room. But we hang there no longer.

Amelia paused, savouring the magical feeling of having the pen in her hand and knowing she was about to write something wonderful with it, even if she didn't know exactly how it was going to come out yet. There were so many things she wanted to say. She wanted to tell about life in the palace. She wanted to tell about each of the princes and princesses who lived there. She wanted to tell about the Shan and the Shanna and the people who served them. All of it seen from above, from the lamp hanging from the ceiling. Amelia could literally *see* it in her mind, as if she were looking down on a scene in the palace below her, even though she had never seen the palace or the people who lived there or anything at all, in fact, from the ceiling of a room. And yet she felt as if she could! She felt as if she had the soul and the mind and the memory of the lamp. Whatever that meant. She felt as if she had opened the tiny door in the panel of the lamp – the one she had tried to open so long before – and now she was sitting inside it. She jumped up and ran out of her room and gazed at the lamp and she *still* felt it! She went back but she didn't close the door, so all she had to do was turn around from her desk to see the lamp whose memory she now inhabited.

She wrote. She wrote about the Shan and Shanna and the princes and princesses and the life of luxury they led in the room below the lamp. She wrote about the joy the lamp felt when the smallest princess gazed up at it with wonder, and when the big man called Ali El lifted her up and helped her find the peacocks and the monkeys and all the animals hidden in its panels. Then she wrote about the night when the princes and princesses ran away and a great crowd of people flooded into the palace, and when she wrote about that, she wrote as if she didn't know what was happening at first, because the lamp wouldn't have known, would it? It had never seen anything like that before, and it wouldn't know that this was a revolution and that its life was going to change forever on that night. Then she wrote about the way someone brought a ladder and climbed up and cut her down, and how the mob pulled her this way and that, threatening to break her glass with its roughness.

Amelia paused again, and gazed at the lamp hanging outside her room. She felt sad. All the other lamps would have been cut down as well. She imagined the scene. All six of the lamps lay on the ground and the mob shouted around them.

'Destroy them! If we can't get the princes and princesses, this'll have to do!'
'Think of all the suffering those people caused us!'
'Smash them up!'
Left and right, the mob began destroying us. Wherever I looked, my brothers and sisters were being smashed. Their glass shattered. Their metal twisted and snapped. But I was

saved. I don't know why. I don't know exactly how. All I
remember is that suddenly someone had me in his arms, and
he was running.

'Take me back!' I cried. 'Let me die with the others!' But
he wouldn't take me back. He ran and ran. Fire was starting
in the palace. I saw others running, carrying things they had
stolen. And then we were outside, in the dark. It was the first
time I had been out of the palace since my maker brought me
there so many years ago. But where was he now? I was alone,
carried away by a strange person, and what would become of
me? At that moment, I wished I had died in the palace with
the others.

Amelia stopped. She could feel the anguish the lamp
must have felt, alone, confused, fearful, torn without
warning from the only home it had ever known, its
brothers and sisters lying smashed and broken in the
ruins of the smoking palace.

But the man who took me did not want me for himself.
He only wanted to sell me to make money. If only he had sold
me back to the man who had created me! But he took me to
a man who bought and sold lamps. Ordinary lamps. He hung me
in his shop. Me! The peacock lamp. A lamp of the palace!
When the other lamps spoke, I ignored them. I was too proud
to speak to them. Some of them teased me. 'Where is your
palace now?' they said. I grew angry. 'Where do you throw

your light now?' they said. But I threw no light. I was dark, hanging on a dark wall, in a small, dark shop. Every day was a torture. Each day was worse than the last. I wished I was dead. That was my only thought. Every hour, every minute, I wished that I had died in the palace with the others.

Eventually a man bought me. He hung me in his house. It was a poor place. The room of the palace in which I had hung was bigger than the whole house. His wife would put one little candle in me, just to see me glow, but she would soon snuff it out, because they didn't have much money and couldn't afford to waste candles. One little candle! The humiliation was almost more than I could bear. I didn't look at what happened beneath me, I didn't care what the man and his wife and their four little children thought when they looked up at me, didn't care if they took pleasure from my glow. Still I had only one thought, to have died with the others in the palace. Then the man got sick, and couldn't work, and his wife had no money, so she sold me back to the man who bought and sold lamps. 'Back again?' asked the others, and I was so angry and humiliated that I couldn't have spoken even if I had wanted to.

Amelia kept writing. From place to place the lamp was sold, and each time the house wasn't good enough for it, too poor, too small, and the lamp hung in angry silence, wishing it was dead, until it was sold again. It never seemed to stay long in one place. Eventually someone bought it and took it across the sea, and the selling began once more. Finally it was brought to a big, green house, and was put up at the very top of the stairs. Even this place wasn't good enough for it, a lamp that had hung in the Grand Palace at Ervahan. But here it stayed, for year after year, until almost fifty years had passed since that terrible night when the palace had been destroyed.

One day the people moved from the green house, but I was left behind, and a new family came. They had a little baby girl. More years passed and she grew older. She was very inquisitive and she would stare at me from the other side of the banister. I didn't know what she wanted. I didn't care. She stared and stared. One day the girl...

Amelia stopped. She turned around and gazed past the open door at the lamp, at the banister below it, remembering that day. She didn't know whether she should tell about what happened next. She didn't know who was going to see this story, or if anyone ever would. And she could always say she had just made it up, and it didn't really happen. Still, she didn't know whether she should say it. Yet she felt she *had* to. The funny thing was, she felt that everything she was writing was the truth, the absolute truth, even though she was making almost all of it up, and if she left out this one thing, this one thing that had actually happened, it would be the only lie in the whole story. And if there was even one lie in the story, the story itself would be worth nothing.

She picked up her pen and continued.

One day the girl tied a rope around her leg and got up on the banister. She put out her hands and grabbed me! Suddenly she jumped off the banister and she was swinging. She swung and swung. Ahhhhhhh! She wanted to kill me. Why? Did she hate me? What had I ever done to her? I could feel my chains straining. They were going to come loose, and I was going to fall all the way down and crash to pieces. She was going to be saved by her rope, and I was going to die. Ahhhhhhh! Ahhhhhhh! Then she jumped off, and somehow I was still there. I hadn't fallen! I was alive!

At that moment, I realised something. I wanted to live! All these years, I wished that I had died with the others in the palace. I must have made that wish millions of times. I thought my life was worse than death. But it wasn't. When I was faced with death, I wanted to live.

The girl didn't swing on me again. The next time I saw her staring at me, I stared back at her. I could see she enjoyed looking at me. I felt something I hadn't felt since those happy days in the palace all those years ago. So much time had passed that I didn't recognise what the feeling was. But it was familiar, it was good. I had felt it before, I knew that.

And then an even stranger thing happened. One day, the

girl brought an old woman to see me. At first I saw her far below, looking up at me from the bottom of the stairs. Then she came all the way up, and she stopped on the other side of the banister. She stared and stared. I stared back. There was something familiar about her, something I knew. And then I had the shock of my life. That face... it was the Princess! The little Princess who had played beneath me in the palace all those years ago, who had looked up at me, who had run her tiny fingers over my panels in the arms of Ali El, who had giggled, who had laughed. The Princess I had last seen looking back at me as she was carried away on that terrible night when the mob came.

But she had changed so much! Not only that she was old, but she was bitter. The kind of person who would walk straight past a girl curtsying on the pavement and not even give her a glance. Was this really the laughing little girl who once had looked up at me with wonder, filling me with delight? She stared at me, and I stared back. And suddenly, I understood. I had become just like her! I had been angry and bitter. In house after house, I had refused to look down, thinking I was too good to be there, thinking the people who took pleasure in me weren't important enough for me to notice. I had become as bitter as the Princess. The bitterness was a poison, and I had poisoned myself.

Suddenly I recognised the feeling I had after the girl swung on me, when I saw her staring at me. It was joy. The joy of giving pleasure to others.

The Princess went away. I was sad for her, but not sorry

to see her go. She wasn't the girl I knew all those years before in the palace, she had changed into someone else. But I had spent enough time poisoning my life. Who could tell when the chains holding me might break and I might smash to pieces? From now on, I would take joy from the pleasure I gave. It didn't matter whether the people who looked at me were princes or paupers. All that mattered was that they enjoyed my glow. I'm a lamp. I was made to give pleasure, I was made to give light. I would never forget that again.

For the first time in fifty-nine years, I was happy.

And a funny thing happened. As soon as I realised that, people started doing things. The lady who lived in the house started doing sculptures of me, although she called them interpretations – which was just as well, because they didn't look very much like me. The man who lived in the house started making strange inventions with light, or trying to, anyway. And another man created a special yoga pose, which was probably the most useful thing of the lot.

But the Princess . . . Well, the Princess, I don't know what became of her. I never saw her again. I wish she could have seen me one more time, now that I was happy. I wish I could have told her what I had finally understood. No one can make you bitter but yourself. I don't know if she could have changed, but if I had been able to tell her that, at least I would have hoped that she could.

But I never got the chance. So I suppose she stayed angry and bitter until the day she died.

It was late when Amelia finished. The time had flown by. She looked at her clock. Time for dinner. Later than time for dinner! Amelia ran downstairs.

Mrs Ellis shook her head as Amelia dashed past the kitchen. 'Just like the parents,' she muttered to herself. 'And I thought *she* was the sensible one!'

Amelia stopped in the doorway to the dining room. Her mother and father were already eating. That was odd. Why hadn't they called her? They always called her. If she wasn't downstairs, one of them, at least, always came up to get her. If the other was sculpting, or inventing, they would join later.

'Reading again?' asked Amelia's father.

Amelia nodded.

'It must have been a very good book,' said Amelia's mother.

Amelia nodded again. She sat down.

'We didn't want to disturb you,' said Amelia's father, 'considering how good the book must have been.'

That had never stopped them before. This was really weird. What was going on?

Mrs Ellis came in with Amelia's soup. 'Reading . . . reading . . .' she muttered, putting the bowl down in front of Amelia. She shook her head disapprovingly, and headed back to the kitchen, still muttering to herself.

Amelia took a mouthful of her soup. Potato and cranberry, one of Mrs Ellis' personal recipes. She glanced at her parents. They both quickly looked away, as if they had been watching her. They couldn't know what she had been doing, could they? They couldn't have sneaked up and secretly opened her door—

Amelia could hardly breathe. The door! She had left it open to see the lamp. She *never* left her door open when she was writing.

She looked at her parents again. Again, they quickly looked away.

Amelia took another spoonful of soup. But she could barely bring herself to swallow. They knew.

She put down her spoon. 'I wasn't reading,' she said quietly.

'Really?' said her father. 'What were you doing?'

Amelia took a deep breath. 'Writing.' She stared at her soup, at the thick, pink liquid, frowning hard. 'I've been writing a story.'

'Well,' said Amelia's father, 'I suppose it's nice to try something new.'

'No. Sometimes . . .' Amelia could hardly bring out the words. But how long was she going to keep covering things up? At least her mother put her sculptures in the garden. At least her father installed his inventions, no matter how useless they were. 'Sometimes I like to write stories,' she said, her voice barely louder than a whisper.

'So this isn't the first?'

Amelia shook her head.

'Well, imagine that! Angeline, did you hear what Amelia just said?'

'I did, Armand,' said Amelia's mother. 'I heard exactly what she said.'

Amelia frowned ever harder.

'Amelia?'

Amelia looked at her mother.

'Are we going to see this excellent story, Amelia?'

'It's just a story,' muttered Amelia.

'I would love to see it.'

Amelia didn't say anything for a moment. She glanced at her father, then back at her mother. 'You don't mind?'

'Mind?' said her mother.

'A Dee has to do something!' exclaimed Amelia's father. 'Invent, sculpt, write. Something!'

'And an Arbuckle, too, Armando,' Amelia's mother reminded him.

'We were starting to get worried,' said Amelia's father.

'Only slightly,' said her mother.

Amelia stared at them in disbelief. 'So you don't think it's . . . silly?'

Amelia's mother and father glanced at each other, and then they both looked back at Amelia questioningly, as if they had no idea what Amelia could possibly mean.

Amelia felt an enormous sense of surprise. And confusion. And relief. And more confusion.

'Well?' said Amelia's father. 'Are we going to read this story?'

Amelia frowned. 'I don't know.'

'Can you tell us what it's called?'

Amelia shook her head. 'I don't know that, either.'

'Perfect!' said Amelia's father. 'Just like me. When I invented my insect powder, I thought it was for sneezes.'

Amelia didn't say anything to that.

'I'm sure Amelia will let us see it,' said Amelia's father.

'I hope so, Armando,' said Amelia's mother.

Amelia couldn't keep herself from smiling. Just slightly.

Amelia really didn't know what she was going to do with the story. She thought about it a lot that night, lay in bed wondering after she turned the light out. It wasn't like the other story, horrible and angry and spiteful, trying to take a revenge it could never take.

Maybe having written it was enough, maybe this one was like all the others and she could put it with them in the drawer and it wouldn't try to get out. But it wasn't meant to stay in the drawer, she knew that. Maybe she could show it to her parents. She wanted to. Now that she had told them, it seemed ridiculous that she had never told them about her stories before. She had always thought it would be so complicated to explain it, and yet it turned out to have been so simple. All her fears proved to be empty. But this story wouldn't mean anything special to them. It would just be a story. There was only one person for whom it would be more than that.

Yet it was one thing to realise that, and another thing actually to give it to the Princess. Had she really written it *for* the Princess? Amelia tried to remember what Mr Vishwanath had said in the conversation that had set off the idea for the story in her mind. Had he said that he thought she could write something better for the Princess, or had he just said that he thought she could write something better? Or both? Or neither? Amelia tried to remember Mr Vishwanath's exact words. But even if she could, she knew, they wouldn't give her the answer. She had to decide for herself. Amelia had come to understand that Mr Vishwanath only asked questions. He never gave answers. Or if he did, even his answers were just another kind of question. The whole point was that his questions were clever enough to make you want to think of an answer for yourself.

Amelia sighed. She knew what she had to do. Deep down, she had known it from the moment she started writing. It was just that the Princess was so haughty, and so stern, and so . . . rude. That was the only word for her. Rude. She had made Amelia feel so small, and she had done it on purpose. Twice. She'd think the story was silly. She'd think that telling a story from inside a lamp was a *fancy*. Amelia could just hear the way the Princess would say it, full of contempt. In her accent. A *fenceee*. Even though Amelia knew perfectly well it wasn't a *fenceee* at all.

The thought of giving the story to the Princess was too scary. Maybe she wouldn't give it to her. Maybe she just wouldn't.

Or maybe there was another way. Mr Vishwanath. He could give it to the Princess for her. Of course! Why not? He saw the Princess all the time.

Amelia was glad she could stop thinking about that and think about the story itself. That was much more fun. She put on the light beside her bed and read it again. When she turned off the light, the sentences ran through her head, almost as if she could see them on a page in front of her. She was so excited about it she couldn't sleep. There were all kinds of things she

193

wanted to improve, all kinds of details, a word here or a sentence there, which is always the way it goes with a story. In fact, the better the story is, and the more you care about it, the more you want to work on it to make it better. And Amelia wanted to work on it, work and work on it, more than anything else she had ever written.

But it needed a title. Amelia thought about that. One possibility after the other ran through her mind, but none of them was quite right. They ran through her mind, over and over, until somehow she fell asleep, still thinking about it. And in the morning, it was the first thing that came into her head as she woke up. But something must have happened in her mind during the night. Because now she knew.

She opened her window and felt the cool morning air on her face. She leaned out and looked at the carved lady. The carved lady looked back with her sightless eyes. Her expression this morning seemed very tranquil, very understanding. Amelia felt very close to the carved lady at that moment. She felt bad that she had ever thought the carved lady looked blank and silly. She wished she could take that back. It had been her anger speaking, it wasn't what she really thought. But she sensed that the carved lady knew it, and had even forgiven her.

'What do you think about the title?' she murmured.

The carved lady stared encouragingly.

'Yes.' Amelia nodded. She went to her desk and picked up her pen. Above the first line of the story she wrote three words.

The Happy Lamp

She gazed at the title for a moment, and then nodded again. Perfect.

She went onto the landing and turned on the lamp. She looked at the glowing metalwork, the two peacocks with their feathers fanning out around the bottom, golden light streaming out of thousands of tiny slivers of space.

'Happy lamp . . .' murmured Amelia Dee, and she smiled.

CHAPTER 22

Mr Vishwanath was in the garden, dressed in his yoga nappy, holding one of his one-legged poses in the sunlight near the lamp sculpture. After a couple of minutes he changed to a different pose, and then held that one. Amelia sat on her chair and waited. There was no way to hurry Mr Vishwanath, she knew.

She got up when he had finished.

'Mr Vishwanath,' she said, as he came towards her, 'I've got something for you.' Amelia held out the pages of the story.

'Is this something else for me to read?'

'No. It's for the Princess.'

'Oh, I thought you said it is for me,' said Mr Vishwanath, and he continued towards the door to his studio.

'Mr Vishwanath!'

He stopped.

'I wondered if you would give it to the Princess,' said Amelia.

Mr Vishwanath smiled. 'Now I understand.'

Amelia smiled as well. She held out the pages again. But Mr Vishwanath didn't take them.

'If you have something to give the Princess, Amelia, you should give it yourself.'

'You mean you won't do it?'

'Why should I do what you can do yourself?'

'Well, it's just the Princess isn't very . . . I mean . . . Mr Vishwanath, you see her anyway. I thought you could just give it to her and say it's from me.'

Mr Vishwanath didn't reply.

'I thought . . .'

Mr Vishwanath shook his head.

Amelia frowned. Deep down, perhaps, she had known this wasn't going to work. She tried one more time. 'Won't you give it to her, Mr Vishwanath? It won't take you long.'

'This isn't the way, Amelia,' said Mr Vishwanath quietly.

'But you don't even know what I'm giving her!'

Mr Vishwanath raised an eyebrow.

'Sorry,' said Amelia. 'It's just . . .'

'What, Amelia?'

'She's so scary!'

Mr Vishwanath smiled. 'No one is truly scary, Amelia. And the most scary people, they themselves are the ones who are the most scared inside.'

Not half as scared as she herself was, thought

Amelia. She looked at Mr Vishwanath doubtfully. 'You took the other story, Mr Vishwanath.'

'That was to read, not to give to the Princess. I will gladly read this one if you want. But I think you don't need me to do that, do you?'

Amelia shook her head.

'No.' Mr Vishwanath chuckled. 'Be brave,' he said, and he went inside, leaving Amelia under the verandah.

She stood there, clutching the pages of the story. From inside the invention shed came a loud pop, followed by a shout of 'Yes!' Then there was another pop, even louder, and this time a shout of 'No!'

Amelia tried to be brave. The next time she saw the cream-coloured car coming down the street she took the story and ran down the stairs and opened the door a fraction and waited for the Princess to appear. But when the Princess actually got out of the car, when Amelia actually saw her there on the pavement, marching past her driver towards the door of Mr Vishwanath's studio with her nose in the air and her black eyebrows fixed in a hawk-like scowl and not the slightest thought for anything around her, Amelia's nerve failed. She could almost hear the words the Princess would utter. 'This is a *fenceeee!* A stupid, stupid story! Why do you give it to me?' Before Amelia knew it, the Princess had gone by and her driver had scurried past her to open the door to Mr Vishwanath's studio, and Amelia herself hadn't even come out of the house.

She felt terrible. She had let herself down. Again. She was a coward.

She hesitated, still peering out the door as the driver passed her on the way back to the car.

'Amelia!'

Amelia jumped. It was Mrs Ellis, in the hall behind her.

'What are you doing there, Amelia? Are you coming in or going out?'

'I'm just . . .'

'Well? Make up your mind.'

'Ummm . . .'

'In or out? Quickly . . . Alright, out you go, then! Go on. Out you go!'

Amelia stepped outside. A moment later, Mrs Ellis closed the door behind her.

Amelia stood there, not knowing what to do next. Was she going to wait here for an hour until the Princess came out? And then what? Run away again?

The cream-coloured car was in front of her. Inside waited the driver, Asha, as he always did.

Of course. Asha . . .

Amelia walked around the car and knocked on the window.

The driver gave a start, but didn't respond.

'I have to talk to you,' said Amelia, pointing at him. For some reason, she mouthed the words, as if he couldn't possibly hear her, although there was only a thin window between them.

Asha shook his head.

'Me . . . You . . .' mouthed Amelia again, pointing. 'Please . . .'

The old man was starting to look very perturbed.

'Pleeeeeeeeease . . .'

Asha looked away in agitation. Amelia watched him beseechingly. She leaned over the front of the car until she caught his eye again. She wouldn't let him ignore her. Finally he opened the door. Amelia stepped back and he got out. Asha straightened up – as much as he could – and very carefully, before he said anything, he put on his hat. Only then, when it was properly adjusted on his head, did he address Amelia.

'Can I help you, Mademoiselle Amelia?'

'You remember my name!' said Amelia in surprise.

'Of course I remember your name, Mademoiselle,' said the old man. 'I must remember all the names, because my mistress forgets.'

'Do you remember my friends?' asked Amelia.

'Mademoiselle Eugenie and Master Kevin.'

Amelia grinned.

'Can I help you, Mademoiselle?' said Asha again. 'This is not usual. I am supposed not to get out of the car. Only for you I do it, Mademoiselle Amelia. Because you insist.'

'Oh.' Amelia was serious again. 'I have something I would like you to give to the Princess.'

Asha looked away uncomfortably.

'Is that a problem?'

'Mademoiselle,' began the old man apologetically. 'I must not take anything for the Princess. It is an iron rule.'

'Sounds like you have a lot of rules.'

Asha shrugged. 'This is a rule, Mademoiselle.'

'Do a lot of people try to give her things?'

'No.'

Amelia frowned. 'Then . . .'

The old man sighed. 'It is a custom from the days when things were different,' he said quietly. 'The Shan and Shanna, her parents, in Irafia they could not take a single step without people trying to give them gifts.'

Amelia understood. In the Princess's world, in the prison she inhabited inside her head, nothing had changed since the moment before the revolution broke out. In reality, no one wanted to give her anything, but by giving instructions to her servant to refuse gifts, she could still pretend that they did.

'It's only a small thing that I want to give her,' said Amelia.

The old man shook his head.

'It's not worth anything. I mean, to buy.'

'I'm sorry,' said the old man.

'Please, sir.'

'Don't call me sir. I am not a sir, Mademoiselle Amelia. I am a servant.'

'Please, Asha. Please.' Amelia kept gazing at him, until he couldn't help but meet her eye. 'Please. For me.'

The old man frowned. 'I have never broken this rule, Mademoiselle Amelia. But for you, because of what you have done . . .'

'What have I done?'

'You think my Princess feels nothing. You think she is as hard, as hard as stone.'

'No,' said Amelia quickly, although that was exactly the way she would have described her.

'She is not like this. Please understand. From the moment she sees the lamp again, something is happening inside her.'

'What?' whispered Amelia.

'I do not know, Mademoiselle. But she is harsh, harsh. Harsher than ever. I know her. For sixty years, I know her. I know what this means, Mademoiselle.'

'Don't call me Mademoiselle. I'm Amelia.'

'But Mademoiselle . . .'

'Amelia. Say it. Please.'

The old man hesitated. 'Amelia. Something is happening inside my Princess.'

'What?'

'Something. I do not know. It is because she sees the lamp.'

Amelia stared. Nothing seemed more important now than to give the Princess the story. She thrust the pages into the old man's hand. 'Give this to her, Asha.'

'What is it?'

'A story.'

The old man frowned.

'Give it to her, Asha. Please. For me.'

Amelia could see the scene clearly. She walked around the corner into Marburg Street. There was the cream-coloured car, and in it the Princess was waiting, as she had waited once before. Asha got out and opened the door for her, and then the Princess got out, and she greeted Amelia, and she was warm, and gentle, and polite, and grateful, and it was all because of the story Amelia had given her. The Princess had changed. It was perfect.

There was only one problem. It didn't happen. The whole scene was in Amelia's imagination. And that was where it stayed.

At first, Amelia really thought it might happen. Every time she came around the corner she expected to see the car waiting. The things Asha had said made her think that something actually was changing inside the Princess. But as the days passed, and the car didn't appear, Amelia realised she was deluding herself. She wondered whether Asha had even given the Princess the story. Maybe he had taken it only in order to get rid of her, and then had thrown it away. Amelia wouldn't have blamed him. After all, if the Princess was harsher than ever, maybe she would fire him if he broke the iron rule about taking gifts for her. And where would he get another job, an old servant like him? Still, Amelia didn't really believe Asha wouldn't keep his word. Much more likely that he had given the story to the Princess, and she had simply ignored it. It seemed ridiculous now to have expected anything else. The Princess had been angry and bitter for fifty-nine years. If something was happening inside her, it was probably just making her *more* angry and bitter.

Amelia licked a Gooseberry and Almond double cone at the Sticky Sunday, thinking about it. Suddenly she was aware that Eugenie and Kevin had stopped talking. She looked around.

'Well?' demanded Eugenie.

'Well what?' asked Amelia.

'You heard me. What do you think?'

'Ummmm . . .'

Kevin grinned. 'I don't think she did hear you.'

Amelia had no idea what Eugenie had just been talking about.

'Well!' said Eugenie, and she put her nose in the air. 'I don't see the point of going out with your friends if you're just going to sit there and think your own thoughts.'

'What am I supposed to be doing?'

'Listening to ours!'

Amelia sighed. The sad thing was that Eugenie probably believed that.

'It's a shame she didn't get on with the Princess,' said Kevin to Amelia. 'They're so well matched, don't you think?'

'I did get on with her!' retorted Eugenie. 'You tell such lies, both of you. To listen to you, you'd think she didn't say a word to me.'

'Eugenie,' said Amelia, 'she *didn't* say a—'

Eugenie's hand shot up, palm out. 'No, I won't listen to that,' she said, and she turned her head, and her nose went even higher in the air, if that was possible.

Kevin looked at Amelia. 'So what were you thinking about just now?'

'Nothing,' said Amelia.

Kevin looked at her sceptically. 'Alright. If that's what you say.'

There was silence. They licked their ice-creams. Or frozen yoghurt, in Eugenie's case.

Amelia stared vacantly out the window. 'Do you think people can change?' she murmured after a while.

Kevin looked out the window. 'Who?'

'No, I mean in general. I don't know. Anyone.'

Kevin frowned. 'I think some people can change.'

'Of course people can change,' snapped Eugenie, who still wasn't really talking to them. Except she couldn't help herself when it came to giving an opinion.

'Like who?' asked Amelia. 'Who do we know who's changed? Come on. Really changed?'

They all thought.

'There was that boy in . . . No, sorry,' said Kevin. 'Forget it.'

There was silence.

'What about Estelle Wesselheimer?' said Eugenie.

'What about Estelle Wesselheimer?'

'She changed.'

'Yeah, but she changed for the worse!' said Kevin.

'No one said she had to change for the better,' replied Eugenie, who was very close to putting her nose back in the air.

'That's true,' said Amelia. 'So does that mean people can change, but not for the better? Is that what we're saying? Can't we think of a single example?'

They all frowned.

'I'm sure we could,' murmured Kevin, 'if we had the time.'

Amelia shook her head. How depressing! They couldn't think of a single kid who had changed for the better. And if kids couldn't change for the better, how much less likely would it be for adults, who were set in their ways?

'Boris Golkov!' said Kevin suddenly. 'He changed!

Boris Golkov used to pull the wings off flies. Do you remember? When we were in grade three.'

'He did,' said Eugenie.

'He doesn't any more.'

'He probably pulls them off birds instead,' said Eugenie.

'No, he's really nice. He doesn't hurt anything.'

'So he changed,' said Amelia. 'Why? What happened?'

'His mum almost died in a car accident,' said Eugenie. 'She was in hospital for months.'

Kevin shook his head. 'That was before he started pulling the wings off flies.'

'It was after.'

'It was before.'

'After!'

'Before!'

'I think it's safe to say none of us knows for certain,' said Amelia.

'I do,' muttered Kevin.

'So do I,' muttered Eugenie.

Amelia sighed. She crunched into her cone. Even if Boris Golkov had changed for the better – and Amelia wasn't certain he had, because she couldn't remember him pulling the wings off flies in the first place – one example of a kid from the third grade was hardly reassuring.

'Why do you ask, anyway?' said Kevin.

'Oh, I was just wondering. You know . . . I was just thinking about the Princess . . .'

'The Princess?' Kevin laughed. 'She'll never change.'

'Never,' said Eugenie.

Amelia looked at them in consternation. 'Why not?'

'She's a bitter old bag. Nothing could change her till the day she dies.'

'She's a princess,' said Eugenie, throwing Kevin a disdainful glance. 'Princesses don't change. They don't need to.'

Kevin rolled his eyes. 'I suppose she told you that, did she? During that conversation you two had? How long did it go on for again? An hour?'

Eugenie put up her hand. She refused to answer.

'I don't know what would have to happen to change someone like the Princess,' said Kevin to Amelia. 'An earthquake, probably.'

'Why should an earthquake change her?' demanded Eugenie.

'You're right,' said Kevin. 'It wouldn't.'

Amelia nodded glumly. It was so discouraging. The truth was so obvious, even Kevin and Eugenie were agreeing! How often did that happen? Amelia felt more ridiculous than ever about expecting the Princess to change, whatever Asha said.

'What do you think someone like that would do if someone did try to change her?' asked Amelia quietly.

Kevin laughed. 'I don't think you'd want to know!'

Eugenie started laughing as well, then suddenly stopped. Her eyes narrowed. 'That isn't what you tried to do, is it?'

'When?' said Amelia, as if she had no idea what Eugenie was talking about.

'The first time you met her. What did happen that day? You never told us.'

'Nothing happened.'

Eugenie looked at her knowingly. 'And the lamp? You never told us how you originally came to tell the Princess about the lamp.'

Kevin nodded. 'That's right. How *did* you come to tell her about the lamp?'

Amelia didn't reply. She had just about made up her mind to tell Eugenie and Kevin that she liked to write stories. After all, she had told her parents, and it had turned out to be a lot simpler than she expected. They actually seemed pleased to hear it. But that was probably because they were her parents. And they weren't the most normal parents in the world, Amelia knew, anyone would have had to admit that. There was no reason to suppose that Kevin and Eugenie would be pleased to hear about her stories. But they wouldn't necessarily laugh at her. And if they did laugh at her, Amelia had decided, that would just show what kind of friends they were.

Still, it was going to take some courage, and it

would be a lot easier if the timing was right. The timing now was just about as wrong as it could be. She had written two stories for the Princess, and each one had just seemed to make the Princess angrier. Telling Eugenie and Kevin about those didn't seem like a great way to start.

They were still watching her.

Amelia got up. 'I'm going home.'

'Are you okay?' said Kevin.

'Yes. I'm just going home.'

She left the shop. Kevin and Eugenie left with her.

'You don't need to come with me.'

'It's alright,' said Kevin.

Amelia glanced at Eugenie, who raised an eyebrow.

Soon they turned the corner into Marburg Street.

Amelia stopped dead. For a second, she was literally rigid. The scene was exactly as she had imagined it.

There was the cream-coloured car, in front of the green house, with Asha in the front seat, and the Princess waiting in the back.

'Amelia,' said Kevin. 'Are you okay?'

Amelia nodded. But her throat was dry. Her stomach had tightened in a knot. This wasn't how it was meant to be, this wasn't how she had imagined herself feeling. But that was because she knew why the Princess was really here. Not for the reasons she had imagined, but to tell her what she thought of her story.

To tell her it was a *fenceee*. To tell her what she thought of her impudence, her sheer cheek, in giving it to her. And then, as a result, to demand to take the lamp back.

And all of this in front of Kevin and Eugenie!

Amelia wanted to turn around and run. But it was too late. Asha had seen them. He was getting out of the car. He was putting on his hat.

CHAPTER 24

The old man straightened up, as much as he could, to face the three children.

'Mademoiselle Amelia Dee,' he announced. 'Her Serenity the Princess Parvin Kha-Douri requests the privilege of seeing the peacock lamp once again.'

Amelia stared.

'She probably wants to make you give it back to her,' whispered Kevin.

'Why not?' whispered Eugenie. 'It's hers really, isn't it?'

'Mademoiselle Amelia?' said Asha. He waited expectantly. There was nothing in his face to show what had happened, if anything, since they last met.

'Yes,' whispered Amelia. She spoke louder. 'Yes, the Princess can see it if she wants. If that's what she wants to do.'

Asha nodded. He walked around the car and opened the back door.

The Princess got out. She glanced at Amelia. Their eyes met.

Eugenie dropped in a curtsy. The Princess walked past her.

Amelia opened the door. Down the hall she went. The Princess followed. Amelia stood aside and waited for the Princess to go up.

'Watch the stairs,' said Amelia. 'The wires . . .'

'Yes, I remember,' said the Princess, and started up the stairs.

They followed her. At the top, the Princess stopped and gazed at the lamp.

Amelia's father came up the stairs, and then Amelia's mother, and then Mrs Ellis, as if the presence of the Princess had somehow communicated itself to every room of the house. Eventually Asha came up the stairs as well, holding his hat.

But no one spoke. Not even Amelia's father.

The Princess continued to stare. The minutes passed. Still the Princess stared.

Finally she murmured something.

'What was that?' whispered Kevin.

'I think she said "happy lamp",' whispered Eugenie.

'What does that mean?'

'I'm not sure *I'm* the one to ask,' replied Eugenie, and she glanced meaningfully at Amelia.

Tears were rolling down the Princess's cheek. 'Happy lamp,' she murmured again.

Suddenly the Princess turned away. She faced the

wall, and put out a hand. Asha gave her a hand-kerchief. The Princess composed herself.

She turned around. She glanced at Amelia, and then started down the stairs.

They all followed.

Outside, on the pavement, the Princess stopped. Asha opened the car door for her, but she didn't get in.

'Master . . .'

'Kevin,' whispered Asha quickly, before the Princess had a chance to say his name even if she could have remembered it.

'Master Kevin,' said the Princess. 'Goodbye. It was a pleasure to meet you.'

Kevin stared at her in surprise. 'Goodbye,' he murmured.

The Princess looked down, where Eugenie was curtsying at her feet.

'Eugenie,' whispered Asha to his mistress.

'Mademoiselle Eugenie,' said the Princess.

Eugenie didn't move. No one could see her face, only the top of her head.

'Mademoiselle Eugenie,' said the Princess again. She reached down and touched Eugenie's elbow. But that wasn't enough either, and the Princess had to grasp Eugenie's arm and almost drag her upright.

Eugenie stared, speechless.

'Do you enjoy meeting princesses?' asked the Princess.

Eugenie's eyes went wider.

'Yes?'

'Yes,' whispered Eugenie.

'You may tell all your friends that I enjoyed meeting you.'

'Yes?' whispered Eugenie.

'Yes,' said the Princess.

Kevin glanced at Amelia and rolled his eyes. Eugenie had already been telling her friends more than that. Just imagine what she was going to say now!

'And a word of advice,' added the Princess, 'when you curtsy, not so long, my dear, nor so deep. A little bob, that's enough. Otherwise it is rather too much, don't you think? Like so.' The Princess bobbed for a second, spreading her arms gracefully, and then was back up again.

Eugenie stared, absolutely dumbstruck.

Then the Princess turned. She looked at Amelia's parents.

Asha began whispering again. 'Madame and Monsieur—'

'I know!' snapped the Princess. 'Do you think I am still a child? Do you think I remember nothing, Asha?'

Asha looked at her in surprise.

'Monsieur and Madame Dee,' said the Princess.

'And Mrs Ellis.' She paused, and glanced triumphantly at Asha, who was visibly astonished. 'Goodbye to you all. I am very glad to have met you again.'

Amelia's father murmured something. Amelia's mother said she was glad to have met the Princess again as well, or something to that effect. Mrs Ellis gave one of her stiff, awkward curtsies.

Then the Princess turned.

'As for you, Mademoiselle . . .'

Amelia winced. Now it was going to start! The Princess had been saving it up, and now she was going to let loose.

'Did you really swing on my lamp?'

'You swung on the lamp?' whispered Amelia's father.

No! Amelia *knew* she shouldn't have put that in. Now the Princess even had a reason to demand the lamp back, because she couldn't trust Amelia to take care of it. And then it would be gone. The peacock lamp. Her lamp. The lamp that contained all her stories, that made her want to write even when she feared that everyone would laugh if they knew.

'I'm glad you did,' said the Princess. 'When I was a little girl, I often imagined doing that. But I didn't have the courage.'

Amelia stared. What was that? What had the Princess just said?

The Princess was watching her. And for the first time – if you exclude the time Amelia had walked in during the middle of her yoga session with Mr Vishwanath, which didn't count because the Princess didn't know she was being observed, and the times when the Princess had stared at the lamp, which didn't count either, because the Princess had been utterly lost in her own memories – her face didn't seem severe. It seemed almost . . . kind.

'I didn't exactly swing on it,' said Amelia. 'I mean, I did, but . . .'

The Princess continued to watch her. There was even a tiny smile on her lips. 'Yes. You made it happy.'

Amelia glanced helplessly at her parents, at Mrs Ellis, who were all staring at her. 'I was trying to get the door open,' she explained, although that didn't exactly answer the question in their eyes.

'And that made it happy?' whispered Kevin. 'What does that mean?'

'When I was a little girl,' said the Princess, 'there was a man called Ali El. His job was to open that little door and light the oil in the lamp every night. He was a giant man, but even he could not reach it, and he would come with a special ladder, and when he stood on that, he could reach it and open the door. Do you remember, Asha?'

'Yes, my Princess.'

218

'One night, after I had asked him and asked him, he held me up so I could see all the little animals in the lamp. The peacocks on the bottom, of course. And the monkeys. Have you found the monkeys in the lamp, Mademoiselle Amelia? You must find the curve of a tail. Find the curve, and follow it, and it will take you to the monkeys.'

Amelia nodded. 'I know.'

'Ah. I couldn't find them at first, but Ali El showed me how. That night, I dreamed about the monkeys, that they came to life and played with me. And the next night, the revolution came and everything was gone.' The Princess frowned, and gave a little shrug, as if there was no other way to express everything that meant. 'That dream, when the monkeys come to life, sometimes I still have it. Even now.'

There was silence.

'Tell me, Mademoiselle Amelia, do you know what is on the top of the lamp?'

Amelia shook her head. 'I've never been able to see.'

'No, I never saw either. I have always wondered.'

'I wonder as well,' said Amelia.

'I am sure one day you will find out. Something tells me that you will.'

Amelia smiled. The Princess smiled as well. At that moment, on the pavement outside the house that Solomon Weiszacker built, the two of them, the girl who lived on Marburg Street and the Princess who had been born sixty-eight years before in a kingdom which no longer existed, shared something that no other two people in the world could have shared.

The Princess nodded to herself. 'May I keep your story, Amelia?'

Amelia nodded.

'You made my lamp happy again.' Tears were starting in the Princess's eyes once more. 'Promise me that you always will.'

'I will,' whispered Amelia. Her eyes were misting as well.

'Mademoiselle Amelia,' said the Princess, 'do you think a person can change?'

'I don't know,' said Amelia. 'I think so. I hope so.'

'Even someone like me?'

'Yes,' said Amelia. Her voice was hoarse. 'Even someone like you.'

'In these last few weeks, I have been thinking. It is not easy but . . . I hope so too. And to hope to do it, that is the first step, don't you think?'

'I think so.'

The Princess stood there a moment longer, gazing intently at Amelia. 'Goodbye, Mademoiselle Amelia. Thank you.'

'Goodbye, Princess,' said Amelia, as the Princess got into the car.

Asha closed the door. He went around to the other side of the car. Then he paused. 'Thank you, Mademoiselle.'

Amelia shook her head. 'Not Mademoiselle, Asha.'

Asha nodded. 'Thank you, Amelia,' he said, and he bowed to her, very smartly despite his age and the bend of his spine, then straightened up, took off his hat, got into the car, and started the engine.

Amelia watched until the car turned the corner.

When she looked around, Kevin was staring at her.

'What's this about a story?'

'I . . .' Amelia hesitated. But it was now or never. And if the Princess had the courage to admit that she wanted to change, surely she could have the courage to admit the truth as well, couldn't she? 'I wrote a story for her,' said Amelia.

Kevin started to laugh.

'Two, actually.' Amelia took a deep breath. So much for choosing her timing. The Princess had chosen it for her. Or her parents would. Amelia could feel them watching her. If she didn't say something, she knew, her father was certain to blurt something out. 'Sometimes I write stories.'

Kevin laughed again. 'Since when?'

'Since . . . for a long time.'

The expression on Kevin's face changed. 'You're serious. Why didn't you ever tell us?'

'Have you ever heard the things you say about Martin Martinez?'

'But that's Martin Martinez! He's always boasting about the stupid stories he's written. He deserves what we say about him. You should have told us, Amelia. We're your friends!'

Amelia looked at him in confusion.

'I bet your stories are way better than Martin Martinez's. Right, Eugenie?'

Eugenie didn't reply.

Kevin looked around. 'Eugenie?'

Eugenie was staring down the street, as if she could still see the cream-coloured car. 'She curtsied to me.'

Kevin rolled his eyes. 'Eugenie, she didn't curtsy to you. She was showing you *how* to curtsy.'

Eugenie sighed. 'She said she enjoyed meeting me, and then she curtsied.'

Kevin turned back to Amelia in disbelief. 'See what you've done?'

Amelia laughed.

'We're never going to hear the end of it!'

Mr Vishwanath was sitting on his chair under the verandah, gazing at the garden. Amelia thought he hadn't even noticed her as she came outside.

'Amelia,' he said.

'Hello, Mr Vishwanath. I didn't want to disturb you.'

'I was hoping you would come. Sit down, Amelia.'

Amelia sat on the chair beside Mr Vishwanath.

'Wait a moment,' he said, and he got up and disappeared into his shop.

Amelia waited. There was a second lamp sculpture in the garden now. You couldn't say exactly what shape it was, except it was all angles and corners, without any of the twisting lines of the first sculpture. When you looked at it from one direction, it looked like one thing, and when you looked at if from another direction, it seemed like another. In an odd kind of way, Amelia liked it.

It was more than a fortnight since the Princess had come to see the lamp for the second time. Afterwards, everyone had wanted to see the story Amelia had given the Princess, but she didn't have a copy, so she had to write it out again from memory. Kevin said it was exceptionally well written, and asked if he could show it to his cousin, Mr Chan, who enjoyed a good story. Eugenie cried at the end, which Amelia took to mean that she thought it was good as well. Then Kevin asked quietly if he could read some of the other stories Amelia had written, but Amelia wasn't sure about that. For about a minute.

Martin Martinez had a competitor now, said Kevin. And about time!

Eugenie, of course, was soon telling stories of her own, mostly about what the Princess had said to her. Apparently, the Princess had stated that she, Eugenie, must really be a princess herself, which is why she had curtsied to her and nobody else, and had said that she must check her family tree carefully to make sure she wasn't the long-lost daughter of some ancient family of royal Edelsteins, and that Eugenie must tell her all about it next time they met. And no doubt Eugenie would be telling even more extravagant stories next week, or the week after. Amelia herself didn't know when she would see the Princess again. But that was alright. Amelia had never really known what effect her story was going to have when she gave it to the Princess. Even if the Princess never came back, she thought, she couldn't have asked for anything more.

Mr Vishwanath returned.

'The Princess gave me something to give to you,' he said.

Amelia looked at him in surprise. 'The Princess?'

Mr Vishwanath held out a small packet wrapped in plain brown paper, tied with a piece of string.

Amelia took it.

'Aren't you going to unwrap it?' asked Mr Vishwanath.

Amelia untied the string and pulled back the paper. Inside was a golden box. It was quite plain, except that in each of its faces was set a small, sparkling jewel. There was a ruby in one, a topaz in another, an emerald in a third and a sapphire in the fourth. And in its lid was set a diamond. Amelia opened it. The box played a mechanical tune. Amelia listened. The tune came to an end. The box itself was empty and lined with black velvet.

Amelia closed the lid.

'It's beautiful,' she said, and she held it out for Mr Vishwanath to take.

'It's for you. The Princess left it for you.'

'I don't understand,' said Amelia.

'She told me to tell you it's the only thing she still has from the Grand Palace. On the night her family fled, this was the only thing she managed to take. She picked it up as she left, and has held on to it ever since, no matter what happened to her.'

Amelia began wrapping it up again. 'I can't take this, Mr Vishwanath. It's all she has left. I have to give it back to her.'

'You can't,' said Mr Vishwanath.

Amelia looked at him in alarm.

'The Princess has gone.'

'Where?'

'To Irafia.'

Amelia stared at Mr Vishwanath. 'When did she go?' she whispered.

'Yesterday.'

'But she's never been back . . .'

'Yes,' said Mr Vishwanath. 'And now she's going. She said it was long enough. She said she wanted to get to know her country again before it is too late.'

Amelia frowned. She gazed at the box. She had told herself it would be alright if she never saw the Princess again, but it didn't feel alright now. And yet, deep down, perhaps Amelia already knew she had seen the Princess for the last time. When the Princess had said goodbye to her on the pavement outside the green house, she hadn't been saying goodbye until the next time they met. She had been saying Goodbye. It was all in the look the Princess had given Amelia before she said it. That look said more than any number of words could have done.

'Amelia, it's good that she has gone back to her

country,' said Mr Vishwanath gently. 'Don't you think it is good?'

'Yes, Mr Vishwanath,' whispered Amelia. 'It's very good.'

It was funny, Amelia found herself feeling sad and happy at once. Yet they weren't different feelings, but two sides of the same feeling.

'She said to ask you to make it happy,' said Mr Vishwanath. 'The box, I mean.'

Amelia smiled. And yet she almost felt like crying as well.

'Do you know what she meant?' asked Mr Vishwanath.

Amelia nodded. She knew what she meant.

There was silence. Amelia wasn't really feeling sad now. She was happy. Happy for the Princess, who had finally gone back to the country from which she had been driven so many years before. Amelia gripped the box in her hand. She would make it happy, she thought, as the Princess had asked.

Suddenly she looked up. 'Mr Vishwanath! That means you've lost one of your customers!'

Mr Vishwanath shrugged.

'And all because of me! I feel terrible!'

'Don't feel terrible,' said Mr Vishwanath. 'I am very happy that the Princess has gone back. For years, I have been trying to get her to do this. Things that seem so complicated, sometimes, when you decide to do them, they are actually very simple. Isn't that right, Amelia?'

Amelia frowned. Those words had a familiar ring. 'Mr Vishwanath . . .' A strange idea came into Amelia's mind. But it was crazy. Or was it? 'Mr Vishwanath, that isn't why you wanted me to meet the Princess, is it? So that something like this would happen?'

'How could I know what would happen when you met her, Amelia?'

'But is that what you hoped? I mean, is that what you . . .' Amelia stopped. It really was a crazy idea. And Mr Vishwanath probably wouldn't answer the question anyway, even if she kept asking. And besides, did it really matter?

'Sometimes you open a door,' said Mr Vishwanath. 'And maybe something will happen. Maybe more than one thing.'

Amelia frowned again. What else was Mr Vishwanath talking about?

Mr Vishwanath smiled. 'Tell me, Amelia, do you think you will write any more stories?'

'People say I should.'

'Really?'

Amelia grinned. 'I think I'd like to write a story about your wild youth, Mr Vishwanath.'

The old yoga maestro chuckled. 'So wild was my youth, Amelia, there is not a story that could compare.'

'Then I'll write a book!'

Mr Vishwanath nodded. 'Maybe one day I will tell you about it.'

'Will you, Mr Vishwanath?'

'Maybe,' murmured Mr Vishwanath.

Amelia waited. But if he was going to tell her about it, he obviously wasn't planning to start today.

'Well, what *are* you going to do, Mr Vishwanath?' said Amelia eventually. 'Seriously. You can't afford to lose a customer. I could make a sign for you. I could put it in your window . . .'

'Amelia, everything will be alright.'

'How do you know?'

'Believe me. Everything will be alright.'

The doorbell in Mr Vishwanath's shop chimed.

Amelia stared at him in amazement. 'Do you think that's a new customer?'

Mr Vishwanath got up to answer it.

Amelia waited in suspense. She turned the box around in her hand. The jewels sparkled.

Mr Vishwanath came back.

'Well?' said Amelia eagerly. 'Was it?'

'Was it what?'

'Don't pretend, Mr Vishwanath! Was it a new customer?'

Mr Vishwanath nodded.

'What happened?'

Mr Vishwanath sat down. 'After I heard what he had to say, I could see he would be happier at Fitness Fanatics.'

'Mr Vishwanath!'

'I would rather have one true student than a hundred followers,' said Mr Vishwanath softly.

'What does that mean, Mr Vishwanath?' said Amelia.

Mr Vishwanath didn't answer. He gazed at the two sculptures in the garden, smiling that smile that was hardly even there.

If you've enjoyed *Amelia Dee and the Peacock Lamp*,
look out for *Antonio S and the Mystery of Theodore Guzman*,
by the same author

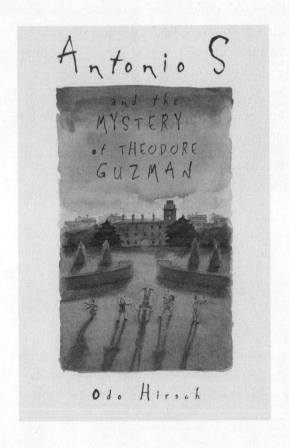

And do you know the Hazel Green books?
Turn over . . .

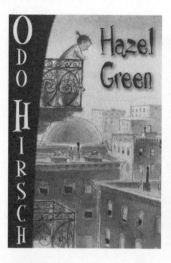

Odo Hirsch — Hazel Green

Odo Hirsch — Something's Fishy, Hazel Green!

Odo Hirsch — Have Courage, Hazel Green!

Odo Hirsch — Think Smart, Hazel Green!